Stolen Sanctuary

A Bindarra Creek Romance

stacey nash

Stolen Sanctuary

ISBN: 0994246684
ISBN-13: 978-0-9942466-8-4

The right of Stacey Nash to be identified as the author of this work has been asserted by her under the *Copyright Amendment (Moral Rights) Act 2000.*

Edited by **Lauren McKellar**
Cover Art by **Stacey Nash**

Dedication

For Suzanne

by Stacey Nash

PROLOGUE

Hangovers sucked. Worse than sucked—they were the hellspawn punishment of the God of Good Times, sent to smite me for not being a good girl. Or so my mother would have said if she knew I'd stayed out all night partying, drinking Sambuca like it was water, and dancing to what she dubbed 'Devil's pop'. I loved the woman dearly, but she needed to get with it; Taylor Swift's older songs were country, not pop, and most of what the band played last night wasn't even new stuff. Not like what the bars back at college played.

I pulled the sleeping bag higher to ward off the morning sun shining through the back window of the car. Pity the soft thud of a headache beat in my ear.

Boom-bah boom-bah boom.

"Morning, sweetheart."

What in God's holy name?

I shot up so fast my vision blurred and my head

spun. Pulling the heavy sleeping bag up to cover my naked—what the hell? *NAKED* breasts—I felt around the hard metal trailer of some stranger's truck until my fingers slipped over the silky fabric of my black dress.

Holy crap, my lady parts were tender as if ...

As if we'd had sex?

Who the hell had I fallen into bed with?

At least I still had knickers on. A low chuckle followed my hurry to yank the dress on without dropping the covers or exposing my too-pale skin to the world. Or the hundreds of people who had turned out to Bindarra Creek's B&S ball last night.

Sheesh.

I'd been happy ... dancing, drinking, singing. *Callie-May.*

Until fricking Callie-May Porter had come along. High school bully and bane of my life, she'd been in fine form last night.

I scooped up my well-loved Doc Martens, and with a hand on the side rail, pushed off and over the side of the high truck bed. Then I fell. Fabric ripped, my palms impacted the cracked dirt, and my forehead followed suit. Holy hot pants. Somehow, in my hasty escape, the dress my friend Savvy had insisted I wear to this thing caught on something and I'd kissed the rock-hard dirt. Stupid drought.

"Are you alright?" His deep voice came from behind me, but I didn't dare look back. Instead, I pushed off the dusty ground, scooped the stupid length of fabric up in my hand, and took off. Shards of rock bit into my poor feet, but I didn't care. That I could handle.

"Hey!"

Pretending I didn't hear whoever he was, I ran until I saw the old Ford I'd borrowed from the Walkers. Something whacked into my back, cascading wet liquid over my butt. Raucous laughter filled the air and a stream of water shot past from the left. I spun around to give the shooter what for, but I wasn't the one in her targets. My foot slipped in the wet and my rear hit the ground, smearing mud all over Savvy's dress.

Pushing myself up, I jumped inside the car. It took a few turns of the key to get the paddock basher to start. The old girl mightn't have been the most reliable, but the loan was a godsend.

I pulled away from the field littered with more sticker-covered trucks and pitched tents than this small country town had ever seen. More smoking hot men and flirty chicks than should ever be in a single place. Ick. I wasn't accustomed to waking up with strange guys; hell, I wasn't accustomed to waking up with any guy, period. I was a virgin for goodness sakes.

Or was I?

Twisting my rear into the cracked leather seat, I clenched my thighs and racked my poor, drink-addled brain. I couldn't remember a darn thing after I started on the Sambuca.

Glancing in my rear-view mirror at the cloud of dust billowing behind me, I breathed a sigh of relief. Maybe my mother's God hadn't smote me after all. It wasn't like I'd ever see that guy again.

ONE

~Three months later~

It was already stifling, even though we were barely into December. Sometimes I forgot how much more extreme everything seemed in the back of nowhere. My phone buzzed against my thigh, and I fell out of step with my mother to flip it open and check the screen.

We made it home in one piece.

Swiping my hand across the sweaty neck of my T-shirt, I smiled at the text from my friend, Savvy. We'd only parted ways for summer break yesterday, but we'd grown kind of close over the past year. I flicked a quick message back her way.

It's going to be a long break. Enjoy yours. Xx

"Put that thing away, Molly."

I rolled my eyes at my mother's back. It'd been three years since I first left for college, but adjusting to being home during breaks was still hard. So many rules. So many perceived niceties to adhere to. So many things my mother deemed sinful. She seemed to think I was closer to two years old than twenty-one.

"And hurry up." She trotted ahead of me, her modest-sized heels clipping against the pavement as we put in long strides to place the Akuna Motel behind us. After all, it was a Sunday at nine in the morning. No one kept the Lord waiting.

Blowing out a breath, I slipped my square flip-phone into the pocket of shoulder bag and spread my toes inside my Docs, then rushed to catch up. Maybe I should have volunteered to man the motel's front desk so Dad could have escorted her to church this morning. That would have given me an out, as well as bonus points. As owner-managers of a small business they never did get a chance to go out together.

A few blocks later, we reached the main street and turned left. The cenotaph towered over the crossroads, and not for the first time I shuddered under its impressive shadow. I'd always been a little scared of the soldier staring down at passers-by. Something about the strong lines of his face, the too-big shape of his arms … Another shudder rippled through me.

My phone buzzed again, and I slipped it out of the shoulder bag thumping against my thigh.

Have a holiday fling, like you did in spring.
That'll make the time go faster.

I spluttered out a laugh. The only guys I was likely

to find around here were either ancient, hillbillies, or taken. Bindarra Creek really wasn't that big, and another one-night stand wasn't exactly on my Things To Do Again list.

My mother spun around, anger burning in her eyes.

"I thought I told you—"

"It's gone." I shut the phone, and pushing it back into the zippered bag, dropped my gaze as we walked onto Willow Tree Circle. BC was such a tiny town it took us all of ten minutes to reach church. There were only one and a half blocks between the motel and Saint James, and all the streets were super wide, none of them with curbs or guttering. The joys of country living. It was funny; my friends from Oxley all called our college town country, but compared to Bindarra, Armidale was a big city. It wasn't until I moved away from BC that I noticed just how quaint my home town really was.

"Who's calling you anyway?"

I flinched out of my own thoughts and met my mother's dark eyes.

"Texting, not calling, and it's a friend."

"Not a boy?"

"So what if it is?"

Denying her a straight answer would rile her up, but frig was I tired of being treated like a child.

"I've warned you—"

"Yes you have." *And I don't care.* Delivered with just the right amount of sass, my words made her stop walking. By now we'd reached St. James and the people milling out front of the sandstone church turned our way. My mother raised a don't-cause-a-scene brow. Dropping her voice to a harsh whisper, she said, "Girls have to be so careful. Even the nice boys are only after …" She bit down on her lip.

"Sex, Mum. Sex." I gritted my teeth. Not that I'd know. I'd only experienced it once and still couldn't remember a darn thing. "Would you prefer it if I was gay?"

She crossed her arms over her chest. "That's not what I said."

"I can't please you." Spinning on the heel of my Docs, I turned back the other way. Spending the morning at church surrounded by all the town gossips wasn't exactly my idea of fun anyway.

"Molly Marie McLean, get back here."

I didn't bother tossing a retort her way. I didn't bother acknowledging the church of the God she so often claimed I'd forsaken; I merely hightailed it down Willow Tree Way with the library in my sights. Just as I reached the path that curled away from the main footpath and in toward the building, a car slowed on the street. I glanced up at the white four-by-four idling on the side of the road. The tinted window slid down to reveal the one church-going woman who I was actually happy to see.

Joy Walker peered out the passenger-side window, a wide smile on her round face, and she pushed her sunnies up into her greying hair.

"Molly dear, I didn't realize you were home."

Sucking back a composing breath, I stepped away from the path and approached the Walkers' car. Waving to both Joy and her husband, Marshall, who sat behind the wheel, I scuffed my boot in the dust.

"I just got back yesterday."

The church bells began to toll. Frowning at the car sitting out front of the police station, I tried to place what about the building had changed. Maybe it was nothing … "Town's looking a little … different."

"Yes, yes." Her eyes lit up with a sparkle. "Thanks to the wonderful work of the Progress Committee, things are looking up for the whole community."

"That's … ahh … great." Did she mean the Save Bindarra Creek group Dad had mentioned last month?

"We'll see you at Bellevue soon then? Marshall can come collect you in the morning."

"Sounds great." Honestly, I'd be glad to get out to the stables and sink my hands into mucking out stalls. Bellevue was the one thing I missed like crazy when I was at Oxley. The horsey company wasn't bad, and the stables themselves were so peaceful. The property had always calmed all the nerves my mother stirred up.

"See you then." Joy offered me a wide smile.

I gave a little wave as she wound up the window and her husband pulled their car into St James' parking lot.

TWO

"You can't just kiss me like that." I tipped my head back to meet his gaze.

"Says who?" His lips parted. "You?"

My head buzzed. My heart thumped as if it were mid-marathon. Even my legs felt kind of weak. He cocked an eyebrow, and his hand slipped up my arm, over my shoulder. His fingers brushed against the thin strap of my dress and trailed over the sensitive skin of my neck, and I shuddered.

With his hand cupping my jaw, he asked again, "You?"

My tongue, huge and wet, refused to work. My tingling mouth couldn't speak. He dipped his head, his lips dusted mine, and I shuddered again. The short pause would have been opportunity to deny him, but I didn't want to. His mouth passed over mine once more then again, the fourth time resting in place. I relaxed a little, drawing the breath I hadn't realised I was detaining.

"No." My admission came on an unsteady exhale.

Then he kissed me so thoroughly my fingers curled into his shirt.

****

Staring at my reflection in the window, I pulled my hair into a braid. Stony eyes looked back, their reflection dulled by the grey parking lot through the pane of glass. Vacant as the upcoming bookings sheet, the lot looked extremely sad. Sadder still was the sound of my parents argument travelling all the way up here to my room. Again. With all signs of the high school sweethearts they claimed to be gone, their bad juju was sucking all the goodness out of being at home. Right then, I would have given anything to fast forward this tense break and get back to Oxley College for my final year. Less than a week into summer holidays meant there were another thirteen weeks to go. Good thing I had Bellevue. The property might not belong to my family anymore, but it still felt like home in a way the motel didn't.

I grabbed a carrot from the fridge and shoved it into my backpack, alongside my lunch. Humming a tune, I walked down the stairs that led to the Akuna Motel's front office. The sound of raised voices hadn't faded. Mostly, the yelling came from my mother. Holding the glass front door with her head stuck out the opening, she shouted, "Water isn't free, David."

I snuck in behind the counter and opened the internet tab on the computer, then typed Facebook's URL into the address bar. The ancient box was more ornament than useful office equipment; proof was in the fact it didn't have the specs to run any decent programs and the little 'thinking' bar was still freaking loading. It was a wonder the stupid thing even had internet access. Meanwhile, water hit the glass window with a loud *whoosh* and my mother pulled her head inside before slamming the door. That sent the bell overhead into a wild dinging. She brushed down her floral print skirt, which did nothing to remove the dark water splats.

Lucky for me, the beat-up paddock basher that belonged to the Walkers pulled up in the prime position, right on cue at seven fifteen a.m. At least I wouldn't have to stick around to hear Mum chewing Dad's ear off over the cost of watering a single flower garden.

Dad disappeared to the side of the window to shut off the hose.

"About time," she muttered, shoving through the hanging bead curtain that covered the entrance into the 'staff only' part of the office, where I stared at the useless cream monitor. I clicked out of the tab that still hadn't loaded, and with a hand on the bright orange counter, I slipped past her outthrust hip as she poured over the booking sheet for the day—no computerised systems here—as though there were something on it.

Pushing through the front door made the bell jingle again, and my dad looked up from recoiling the hose, offering me a wink. "Have a good day, honey."

"Mind you don't drown those plants." Suppressing my smirk was harder than expected. Dad didn't even try to hide his and worse yet, he made as if to grab the hose again, totally ignoring Mum's scowling face behind the window.

Marshall smiled a hello as I climbed in the passenger seat. "Buckle up, buttercup."

I shook my head at the phrase he'd said every time

I got in his car. And that was mighty often. I'd been working in the stables since the Walkers bought my pop's land when I was barely a teenager. New to the countryside, Joy and Marshall hadn't known an awful lot about horses and so had asked me to help out. After I'd moved away to Oxley, it was always a given I'd be out at Bellevue when I was home, and since I'd left, Joy had been more like a surrogate mum than a boss, checking in with me every other week.

As we drove past the cenotaph, Marshall asked, "How's school?"

"Oh, you know ... all study no play."

He raised a brow without looking my way.

"Well, a little play."

The side of his mouth twitched up.

We turned onto the road that led out of town and the mountains on the horizon drew my gaze. Surrounded by rolling hills that pointed toward the lone range, Bellevue was easy to spot. A little way along the road after crossing the creek, Marshall swung the old Ford into the driveway of Bellevue Stables. Or so said the fancy lettering emblazoned on the wooden fence palings framing the entry.

"That's new."

"A little over the top, but Joy likes it."

Rattles shook the old car as we crossed the iron grate. A dirt road wound up the hill past the main homestead, and I couldn't help admiring the whitewashed structure that had once belonged to my grandparents. An old house that dated back to heritage times, it still looked pretty good. The huge Moreton Bay fig out front stood guard over the property as if it were a sentinel against the scorching summer sun. I'd spent many summers in the branches of the grand tree when I was younger. Sighing, I pulled my attention to the much newer structure of 'the stables'. At roughly fifty years old, they were built by my pop in his younger days as a way to house all the ponies the townsfolk didn't have the space to keep.

Just as well-kept as the main homestead, the wood-plank stables were large enough to house at least a dozen horses. Another half dozen usually roamed the east paddock, but these days, the back paddock was strictly out of bounds. That little slice of land still belonged to my family. More specifically to me, or at least it would when I turned twenty-five.

Climbing out of the car, I sucked in a deep breath of country goodness. Amazing how the smell of horses and tack and hay felt like it had settled into my blood. Marshall smiled, as if he knew just how I felt. He closed the creaky car door and tossed me the keys to the Ford, which I caught out of the air with a "thanks."

For the past few summers when I'd been home, they'd loaned me *the basher*. It saved one of them driving me to and from Bellevue each day, or worse yet, me relying on my folks. Mum's car would just chew through petrol that cost more than water, or so she complained. At least I could keep the basher topped up without her having any input. I shoved the keys into the front pocket of my backpack and, not needing instruction, made for the swung open barn doors and walked inside. The smell of hay was twice as strong in there, and I smiled at the memory of times bygone with my pop. I'd tagged along while he mucked out stalls, checked on horses, mixed chaff, and exercised his ponies.

The first stop I made was at the third stall on the right, but when I leaned over the gate the space smelled musty, as if it hadn't been used in some time. Frowning, I leaned back to look at the horseshoe hanging over the stall; the nameplate on it still read Jed. Not that it meant a lot, as none of the nameplates had changed in … well, since I was thirteen. He was probably in the east paddock.

A soft whinny came from the opposite stall, and I stopped to rub Angel's nose on my way to the little back room where I dumped my bag. 'The office' felt somehow different, not that I could place what made the room not quite the same. Dust still covered every surface, piles of papers and files lined the walls, and the photo board looked exactly the same, hanging beneath the line of name plaques.

My usual day at Bellevue started with mixing up chaff and grain, so I headed to the store room and did just that. It took most of the morning to make the rounds, feeding the ponies and mucking out the stalls, then giving them each a generous rub down after my three-month absence. Not that there were many horses. The past few years there seemed to be fewer inmates. People didn't keep horses as much these days.

When all the work was done, I retrieved the carrot I'd placed in my bag that morning and went in search of my ex-race horse. Years ago, Pop had saved Jed from slaughter and even though I was far too short for the gigantic sixteen-hand grey, I'd begged for him to be mine. It took until I was fifteen for me to be able to hoist myself onto his high back and even now, if I rode without a saddle I had to lead him up beside a chair. Thankfully, Marshall had let me keep him here since they took over the property, and wouldn't accept any payment for his agistment, even though they paid me nicely for the work I did around the place.

It turned out Jed was in the east paddock, grazing away with a handful of other horses. When I called his name, he raised his head and looked my way. He didn't make my job easy, but rather dropped his nose back to the lush grass. By the time I trudged the three hundred odd metres to where he stood, he hadn't so much as moved an inch.

"Hey there." I reached out a hand and Jed nudged my fingers with his soft nose, no doubt in search of his treat. "You got me." Smiling, I pulled the carrot out from behind my back and held it tight while he bit into it. He devoured the whole thing in two bites. After he'd finished chewing, I slipped a bridle over his lowered head and led my horse back to the stables, where I grabbed my backpack and saddled up the grey gelding. All the work was already done, but I wasn't ready to head home yet, so with the bag on my back, I heaved myself up and threw a leg over his back. Eager for a run, Jed took off at a trot with no more encouragement than a nudge.

As soon as we were out of range of the building, I loosened the reins and let him go. Taking my cue, Jed picked up his pace to a fast trot that opened into a full-on canter. I whooped as the air hit my face, blowing my hair out behind me. There was nothing better than the first ride after being away all school term, and my retired racer seemed to agree. By the time we reached the gate that separated Bellevue from the back paddock, my cheeks felt a little achy, either from grinning or the blast of wind against them, I couldn't be sure.

Walking Jed up beside the gate, I reached down and unhooked the latch then, in a well practiced move, had him walk us through while I twisted around, gate still in hand, to pull it closed behind us. As soon as the latch was back on its holder I let my gentle giant know he could take off. We galloped the couple of hundred metres it took to reach the steady incline that led to my favourite place on this entire property. Jed slowed, knowing the routine we'd followed so many times before. He knew I liked to dawdle on the last leg of our ride in order to suck up every iota of enjoyment the picturesque landscape offered. A thick copse of trees marked the line where Bindarra Creek wound its lazy way through the corner of the last of this land my family still owned. Throwing a leg over the side of my stockman's saddle, I slid down off Jed, my feet thudding onto the ground.

I pulled the reins up and over his head, then led the big grey toward my treasured spot. The place I'd put in many hours when life handed out lemons, which during my high school years had been often enough. I glanced down at my chunky thighs ... thankfully I'd moved away from this town and Callie-May Porter's exclusive clique.

Three steps shy of reaching my destination, I stopped short. An intruder sat on the huge flat rock that overlooked the widest part of the creek. His arms were pitched back on the boulder and his legs kicked out to full length, his wide-brimmed Akubra hat blocking his face from view.

My heart clenched at his invasion on my turf, and as if Jed sensed the sudden shift in my mood, he let out a questioning grunt.

Without moving from his relaxed pose, the stranger glanced over his shoulder, and my throat squeezed in on itself. As good looking as anything, he had to be around my age, yet I'd never seen his face before. He certainly hadn't been among the twenty-two graduates in my senior class. I'd remember that half-cocked smile. Those unusual smoke-coloured eyes. That perfectly square jaw.

Lifting a hand, he tipped the front of his hat and spun around, pushing up off *my* rock.

"Who are you?" I asked.

He watched me, watching him. "Who are you?"

Heat engulfed my face, my neck, and I stammered, unable to form a damn sentence. Why was I so freaking backward? It was alright if I was talking to guys who posed no threat, like my friends' boyfriends, but guys like this, who were hotter than even Savvy or Olivia's men, they reverted me back to toddlerhood.

"This … this is private property."

He raised a brow. "That so?"

"You're trespassing."

Turning his back on me, he dropped into his earlier pose and tipped the hat down over his face.

"Aren't you going to leave?"

"Nope."

Jed's reins slipped through my fingers, and I rushed to scoop them up, then buckled the leather straps around a low tree branch. Mr Mysterious didn't move; he didn't even pretend to care.

"You can't be here."

"Says who?"

I stood there staring at the back of the stranger's arrogant head. Jed nudged my shoulder, pushing me forward, and my balance tipped. I stumbled, my feet struggling to gain purchase, and I muttered, "Stay out of this, horse."

By all accounts the stranger seemed to have returned to his nap, oblivious to my little display of unco-ordination. I adjusted the straps on my backpack and climbed back onto the grey, tugging his head up from grazing with a tad more force than was strictly needed. Jed took the cue and turned, taking off up the creek without any encouragement.

Trespassers, no matter how good looking, weren't welcome. This was the one place I loved more anything else, and the only spot where the rest of the world faded away.

THREE

Hot lips danced on mine. My hips ground against his to the beat of the music. Fire flowed through my veins, and I felt as if I had lost control. Need had taken over and I needed this, needed him, needed to feel. There was something about this guy that was utterly desirable. No other word could describe it.

Perhaps it was my Sambuca buzz. Shit am I drunk? I couldn't—

Firm hands cupped my thighs as I jumped up, my feet linking behind a solid back, resting on the curve of his firm butt. I shouldn't—

"I'm not. I can't—"

Hooking up with a total stranger was so sleazy.

He pulled away enough to look me in the eye for a few heartbeats. His grip on me loosened and everything inside me screamed 'No, don't let this end.' I slammed my needy lips back against his and clenched my legs around his middle.

Returning my kiss with just as much force, he backed us away from the main marquee and my blood roared its approval.

****

Dragging the handful of items out of my basket, I threw them onto the counter at our local supermarket. A packet of salt and vinegar chips for Dad, fresh bread for today's lunch, and some batteries to feed my archaic CD player.

The young girl on the counter rang them up, and I paid with the cash I'd grabbed from Dad on my way out. Just as she bagged the order and handed it over, old biddy and town gossip extraordinaire Pamela Brown bustled through the front door. I ducked my head, hoping for a swift exit.

"Molly McLean. Is it that time of year already?"

Too slow. "Hello, Mrs Brown."

"You're home from school?"

"Yes, it is almost Christmas." I smiled, shifting my load to the other hand.

"How are your parents doing, pet? With all the new competition in town, I'd imagine business is tough."

"New business ..." This woman always caught me off-guard.

"Tess and Dodge's lodge. The way they've set that place up ... it's just beautiful. Why anyone would want to stay at a rundown motel when there's a newly renovated bed and breakfast on offer is a fine question." She smiled as if she were proud. "Perhaps your folks should look at tidying the old motel up." Her thin shoulders squared. "And the plans for the rooms above the Royal Hotel? Oh my, they're set to be stunning. Oh, and dear, have you been out to ..."

Things had always been tight for my family. Not many visitors came to our little town. Bindarra Creek wasn't on one of the highways that led to a state capital, or even a large city. Pretty much the only people who passed through were those on business and those visiting family who didn't have room to put them up. How a town with a grand population of 2079 was going to support a host of accommodation businesses was a mystery to me. No wonder my mother's moods were more rocky than normal.

Still talking, old Mrs Brown squeezed my arm. "Isn't that right, dear?"

With no idea what she'd asked me, I nodded. "Yes, that's right. Excuse me." I stepped to the side and around her. "It was nice bumping into you."

"Take care, lovie."

I rushed out the front door before she thought of another revamped place that would directly affect my family's livelihood. This whole Save Bindarra Creek movement was a good thing for the town, but I wasn't too sure how good it would be for my family. Once outside, I slowed the pace, avoiding the piercing gaze of the solider on the cenotaph as I skipped my turnoff and walked half a block out of my way to check out the Royal Hotel. The old pub looked pretty well the same way it always had—a sandstone base topped with dark bricks and faded wooden double doors. A cacophony of noise came from inside, so maybe old Pamela was right; the place was undergoing renovations. I crossed the deserted road to sneak a look, but as I drew closer a sheet of paper pasted in the window caught my eye.

Bushman's Ball.

Hmm, that was new. *Christmas Eve, bring the whole family for a fun night at the soon-to-be renovated Riverside Hotel.* Riverside? I glanced up at the inscription marking the top of the pub, but of course was too close to see, so I returned my attention to the flyer. *Enjoy the night, while supporting local improvements.*

I crossed back to the other side of the street, glancing up at the facade that read *Royal Hotel, est. 1913.* Guess they hadn't swapped names after all. Pamela must have gotten muddled. It'd be the Riverside renovating rooms, but why on earth would the Royal be advertising for them? And what the heck was with all the noise ... it wasn't like it was a Saturday night in Armidale. Bindarra Creek was sleepier than Oxley College at 9 a.m. on a Sunday morning.

I pulled my ancient phone out of my pocket and sent a text to each of my girlfriends as I walked home. This was the third summer I'd spent in Bindarra since moving away, but I hadn't really felt loneliness until this year.

By the time I reached Akuna's covered driveway, neither of the girls had answered and Pamela's claims of bad business had coated my tongue in a sour taste. I pushed through the front door to the jingle of the bell overhead, and my dad looked up from where he sat behind the front desk, reading today's newspaper. Suddenly, the beige shag pile and matching velvet drapes with dusty lace under-curtains felt dated. Even the plant hanging from its macramé noose with its festive tinsel felt somehow different, as did the bauble-covered Chinese Money Tree sitting on the corner of the high counter. It was like I was looking at the front office with a new outlook. Dad licked his finger and used the damp digit to turn the page of his paper. I glanced at the ever-silent phone. The red light was on, so the batteries were working.

"Is business bad?"

Dad closed the paper and pushed it aside, looking around the makeshift Christmas tree.

"Why do you ask?"

I waved toward the deserted parking lot. "It seems quieter than usual."

His cheeks puffed up then he blew out a long breath, ruffling the red tinsel lining the counter. "Don't you worry about how things are doing here. You just concentrate on that course you're doing so well with."

"Do ... do you think maybe the Fig Tree Lodge has affected our bookings? Or the Riverside Hotel? Everyone's doing all these great renovations and ... This time of year is usually a bit busier." I glanced around the small office and scratched an itch near my ear. "Maybe we should make a few changes, too. Pretty the place up a bit."

"And where are we going to get the money for that?" I hadn't noticed my mother standing at the entry to our upstairs quarters.

Using the counter for purchase, Dad pushed up off his stool. "The style hasn't been updated since the 80s, Patty."

"And the decor is still as good as when it was new."

I threw my hands up in a gesture of peacekeeping. "It was just a thought. Maybe a way to keep our guests loyal."

"Molly has a fair point." Dad gestured my way, and I tossed him the packet of chips he'd requested, just clearing the little tree.

Mum stepped delicately down the stairs as I made my way up. "Molly has no idea what she's talking about. There are several reservations tonight. The tradesmen that are working on the Riverview will be here and why, that gentleman walked in off the street just the other day. I don't think—"

I shut the door, blocking out her voice. Deny as she might, business *was* bad. We'd always struggled a little more than most families, but ends had never failed to meet, and if it was this quiet over summer then soon those ends might not come together at all. I placed the shopping bag on the bench and retreated to my room, where I threw yesterday's horsey jeans into my backpack for the ride I might sneak in later this afternoon. After slapping together a sandwich, grabbing an apple for Jed and a huge bottle of water for me, I ducked back downstairs. My parents were still at it, but I didn't bother stopping to hear Mum's reservations. Instead, I pushed through the door and hopped in the basher. The engine took a little coaxing, but finally turned over and I was off, more than ready to forget about this place for a few hours.

The old Ford shuddered up Bellevue's driveway, and I noticed what I hadn't the day before. Some kind of crop filled half the west paddock. Not that it was unusual. My pop had farmed the land, running the stables as a sideline, and Marshall had tried his hand at lucerne hay more than once. I'd just never seen actual plants ... like watermelon, maybe ... growing in the ploughed soil.

I parked in my usual spot, right under the huge gum tree which threw shade onto the stables in the early afternoon. That should ensure the basher didn't turn into an oven while I worked. Over toward the exercise ring, an Akubra-wearing figure caught my gaze. Putting a young horse through its paces, yesterday's trespasser lunged forward and back with a certain grace. Even from here I could tell those jean-clad legs were strong, as were the broad muscles across his impressive shoulders. The young chestnut ran the circle, never failing to miss a transition.

"Not bad with her, is he?"

I jumped a little, heat flushing my cheeks as I rubbed at my ear. "Ah, yeah."

"Have you two met yet? Callan's our nephew."

Holding a paper bag in her right hand, Joy Walker stood beside me. A little older than my own parents, Joy had a certain charm that often had me confiding in her over the years. Even so, there was no way I'd tell her about the thoughts I had when it came to the hot guy out there working with her young filly. Swooning over boys was not my style.

"Umm ..."

Joy nudged me with her elbow. "Come, I was taking him a snack anyway. Let's say hello."

I took a step back toward the barn. "I'm ... ah ... running late. Got to give the inmates breakfast and umm ... Angel's hooves need a little care. The front right looks like it might split, and Flash has some kind of mite—"

"Molly," Joy said. "Callan won't bite."

I swallowed the thick feeling in my throat, and Joy pushed her sunglasses onto her head. She studied me, her kind eyes somehow softer than usual, and I nipped the corner of my lip. "Sure."

Her concern melted instantly, and grinning, the older woman took my arm and led me across the field. Callan didn't slow the young filly down, nor did he stop working. He did, however, tip his chin toward us.

Joy pressed her arms against the top rail of the

exercise yard, the paper bag dangling from her fingers. "He just finished up a business degree majoring in Hospitality Management at UQ, while he worked in a retreat up in the Hinterlands. Marshall thought a bit of country air might be just what he needed before diving into the workforce."

I *hmm*ed my agreement, watching as Callan wound the young horse down from her workout. Joy was right; he sure was good with her. The way he moved was almost graceful, if that word could be used to describe thick thighs and flexing muscles. Nonetheless, his lunges, steps, and sweeps were beautiful.

"Molly."

Joy's gentle nudge brought me back to the moment, and I found myself looking up into a deep grey gaze. My face burst into a scorching blush.

"Molly," Joy said my name again, and I noticed an impressively large hand extended between the rails.

Holding my breath, I grasped his hand and shook once then let go.

He smiled that arrogant half-smile from yesterday, and it was so sexy I melted from the inside out. "I'm Callan."

"Molly." I tried to return his smile.

"I know."

Heat flooded my face again, and I dropped my gaze to the toes of my Docs.

"I—I've got to get to work." Without waiting for a response, I turned and fled for the safety of the stables. I get tongue-tied easily, but I didn't usually swoon. Something about this guy undid me.

****

I seemed to zoom through the chores, even managing to file back Angel's hooves and get some powder on Flash's mites before midday. Hopefully I'd gotten the parasites in time and they hadn't spread to any of the other horses. For some reason though, my nerves were shot. I dropped an entire feeder box of chaff all over the store room, bumped into every single support post I walked past, and fumbled the apple I'd brought for Jed, dropping it in his water bowl as I was passing it to him. So much for Bellevue being my sanctuary; today it was more like a china shop that needed to safety-proofed.

When all the inside chores had been done, the only thing left to do was switch a few horses out to the east paddock for the day. I threw a halter on the little mountain pony—she was the only horse in here other than the young filly, the two sick horses and Jed—and led her outside. The little pony's ears pricked up, and she swung her head from side to side as she picked up the pace, clearly excited to be out.

Letting her trot up beside me, I gave the little gal a pat on her neck, and that was when I saw *him* again. With a clipboard in hand, Callan pointed toward the back paddock, and the suit-wearing man beside him nodded. They walked across the field, stopping every so often to prod at the ground, all the while the important-looking man scrawled in his notebook and punched at the phone in his hand.

Squatting in the long grass, Callan hammered something into the ground. The T-shirt he wore, though reasonably loose, didn't fail to show off the impressive bulge of his biceps as he worked. A got a good look in as that cowboy hat blocked his face from view.

Neither man paid me a lick of attention as I walked the pony through their space.

"What's happening with the pillar and plank eyesore?" Suit guy waved toward the stables and I glanced back that way, looking for something ugly.

Callan mumbled something I couldn't hear properly, and the man nodded, then pinched his jaw. "You do realise ..." The rest of their conversation floated away on the gusty westerly that chose that moment to pick up.

I pitched forward, pulled along by the excitable bay pony.

"Alright already," I grumbled, leading her through the gate and into the east paddock where I slipped her halter off and gave her a soft slap on the rump by way of farewell. The pint-sized mare took off, kicking her back legs in the air as she ran right toward a bunch of old car tyres. Off to the side of the paddock and piled on top of each other, they formed a rubber mountain. Perhaps Joy was going to set up some jumps, or host an upcoming pony club meet. Pop would most certainly have approved of that.

When I turned back, the two men were walking around the exercise yard, pushing on the rails as if to check their sturdiness. What was Callan up to? That other man seemed like he was a businessman, but asking about the stables and plans for them ...

I took my time returning, stopping to pluck a few wild dandelions along the way. When I next looked Callan's way, he was walking the other man toward a four-wheel drive parked right next to the basher. They shook hands, and the suited dude stepped up into his truck. While I was walking toward the stables, the SUV reversed out from under the huge gum and turned a full circle. The manoeuvre showed off the Signage stretched along the entire driver's side of the white car—*Bindarra Building Company*.

Dread pooled in the pit of my stomach.

Taking long strides, my feet slammed against the dry ground and the dandelions fell through my fingers.

Callan lifted a hand as the car disappeared down the drive in a cloud of dust, then smiling, he turned to face me. I strode right up to him, and for the first time since I'd met him words didn't fail me. "What the hell is going on?"

Callan raised his brows and his lips twitched as he shoved a hand in his jeans pocket. The other hand tipped his hat up, revealing his smoky eyes. "Change."

"What type of change?" My eyes slipped to the building behind him, and Callan tipped his hat back down.

"The good type." He turned, walking inside the well-built stables. His boots kicked up the dust and I coughed, watching his arrogant arse leave.

Snapping back to my senses, I followed.

"These stables are solid and strong. There's nothing wrong with them. We have plenty of stalls to fill—"

He swung around and I took a step forward, moving into his space. We were almost eye to eye and there was a certain fire in his, like he was challenging me. A freckle danced just under his left eye as his gaze dropped to my chest for the briefest of moments. Everything inside me screamed to step away, but I couldn't back down. When his eyes returned to mine, heat pooled low in my belly and oh no, I couldn't want him. Not like that. Not now. Especially not after he'd just so blatantly checked out my boobs. Since my one-night stand at the B&S, the flood gates to my lust-o-meter were wide open.

I swallowed against the sudden flood in my mouth, and Callan stepped forward so we were close enough that I could hear the steady tick of his watch, could taste his exhale on the air I breathed in.

"Marshall and Joy hired me to make this place a more viable business, and that's exactly what I'm going to do."

His eyes stared into mine with so much heat that I feared the straw lining Jed's stall might burst into flames. With no warning, Callan stepped back, turned and walked away. My knees weakened, and I grabbed the side of my horse's stall to keep from toppling over. What in God's name was wrong with me?

This business mightn't be my grandfather's anymore, but that didn't mean it needed any changes that risked knocking down what he'd built with his bare hands. I loved Joy and Marshall, but Mum never should have sold this land. Pop had wanted me to take over his business when I was old enough. That was why he'd left me part of the property in trust.

Bellevue was a viable business ... there was horse agistment and stables and ... and ... and growing watermelons. Callan Hunter had no idea what he was talking about.

FOUR

It was only two p.m. when I steered the rust-filled basher into the parking lot of the Akuna Motel. I swung the door open, pocketed my keys, and climbed out into the warm December air. Sweat dribbled down my back, but the cause wasn't this weather. I was still hot under the collar from the run-in with Callan. Something about that guy ticked every box that made up the lust list I hadn't realised I owned. I'd never really considered what I found attractive in a guy, and still didn't exactly know, but somehow Callan had it pegged, and geez did he know it.

I twisted my shirt to get comfortable, but the thin fabric itched and stuck to my skin.

"There's just no way, David."

I inhaled through my nose, exhaled through my mouth, and braced myself then pushed through the glass door that led into the front office.

"Three months in arrears, and look here." A *thud, thud, thud* marked my mother's violent finger-stabbing of something on the desk. "In the red."

She glanced up, saw it was just me and resumed pouring over the papers, so I moved around the side of the counter, with reaching the upstairs door that stood behind them my objective.

"Molly, how was the farm?" Dad glanced away from the paperwork spread over the entire length of the bright orange counter. Creases lined his forehead, and pink splashed his cheeks. My mother's plaid dress swayed as she moved between two piles of papers.

"Alright, I guess." Sweat covered my back, my brow too, and I wiped it away with my fingers. Holy crap, it was hot in here. "Did you know the Walkers' nephew is staying with them?"

Mum's head snapped up, her bobbed hair whipping around her face. "You be careful around him."

Lecture time—here we go. I cocked my head to the side. "Have you met Callan?"

"He's a young man, Molly. I don't need to meet him to understand him."

Dad shook his head. "I'm sure he's a good kid, Patty."

Taking the moment's distraction Dad had brought me, I slipped up the stairs and through the door. My jeans felt like they were made of polar fleece or maybe lined with eiderdown, so going straight to my room, I kicked off my shoes then peeled the sticky pants off. I threw on a pair of cotton shorts, then changed my T-shirt, too. As much as I loved the horses, smelling like them for the rest of the day wasn't pleasant. A shower could wait until after lunch.

I gathered up the keys to the basher before I lost them and shoved them into my pocket, then fished the warm sandwich out of my backpack and screwed up my nose at the melted butter/vegemite combo which I hadn't found the time to eat. That belonged in the bin, which was exactly where I tossed it before making myself a nice cool cucumber sandwich on this morning's fresh bread. I poured myself a glass of ice water, threw back the freezing liquid, then rolled the cool glass across my forehead.

It had to be hotter in here than it was outside. Mum and Dad mustn't have had the air on. I went across the room to near the TV, where the air-conditioning remote lived, but the little holder on the wall was empty. A check of the coffee table, the kitchen bench and the fruit bowl produced nothing. The darn thing wasn't anywhere.

Having worked up even more of a sweat, I dumped the empty glass that was now as warm as my scorching skin and threw open the door to the motel.

"Anyone seen the air-con remote?"

Dad's flushed face rose from the papers that were now spread across the floor as well as the bench, and my mother snapped, "We don't need air-con. It's not hot."

"Are you kidding me? I'm losing so much sweat I'm dehydrating up here."

"Then drink some water."

I pulled the door closed behind me and trudged down the four stairs, checking out whatever they were working on.

Bills.

Covering every surface of the office. Power, water, linen service, milkman, confectionary, council rates—even the local library had sent an account for overdue books. There were so many bills that the little

Christmas/money tree had been shoved into a corner to make space.

"In this order ..." my mother counted off on her fingers. "We can't operate without power or water. The council rates will need to wait."

The bell set off ringing, announcing an arrival, and my parents both looked up. A man wearing workman's overalls stood in the entry. "I've got three rooms for tonight. Booking should be under Stanley Constructions."

"Of course." Mum smiled, and Dad gathered up all the accounts, shoving them into a tray under the counter, then he left the office while Mum checked in the arriving guest. I followed Dad out into the parking lot and caught him up somewhere around room five.

"Look, Dad, things are obviously really tight. The money I earn helping out at Bellevue—"

He glanced across at me as we walked along the covered footpath which connected the back rooms to the front. "Don't even finish that sentence. Yes, money's tight right now, but we'll pull through, so don't worry about this place."

"If you won't take it for bills, what about for improvements? We could—"

"Molly, we're not taking your college funds."

I huffed out a sigh. "With a hundred dollars, we could paint this pavement."

He glanced down at the peeling green paint and wiped a hand across his brow. "Sweetheart, your heart's in the right place, and I love you for that, but no."

Another sigh and this time I turned around. I scuffed my bare feet against the splotchy concrete as I headed back toward the office. At least it felt coolish under my toes. My parents clearly needed to do something, but I'd be stuffed if I knew how to help.

The bell jingled as I reached for the front door, but the builder beat me to it, holding the glass open. I stepped to the side, allowing him to exit the office, but he smiled and said, "Ladies first."

His smile never faded as his gaze dipped to my chest. Blushing, I twisted my arms across the boobs that always drew attention and walked through the door with a muttered, "Thanks."

A low whistle came before the jangle of the bell and my mother shot up off the stool behind the counter and pushed me out of the way as she rushed toward the motel's entrance, which she reefed open. Sticking her head out, she shouted, "There's been a mistake. We're full tonight."

She just said *what?*

I pushed through the door. "No, we're not. There isn't a single other booking."

The man looked from her to me and shook his head. "Well, what is it? Have you got rooms or not?"

"Not," my mother snapped, then turned to me. "Go upstairs."

"What?"

"I said, go inside."

"What the hell, Mum?"

She shoved me through the door and yanked it closed, trapping me inside the office. Through the glass I saw her approach the man she was apparently kicking out, his booking details in hand. She tore then tossed, sending little scraps of paper fluttering to the ground. With the exit no longer barred by my mother, I pushed through the damn door again, but it was too late. He was already in his ute, the vehicle pulling out of our parking lot.

"What in the hell?" I said again.

She turned on me. "Watch your language, Molly."

"You just kicked out a paying customer. Three, actually."

She looked at me and shook her head. "You need to learn how to read men. I sure hope you manage better than this at college."

I stepped back, and my head smacked into the macramé hanging pot.

"He was ogling you. We don't need his kind around here."

"Far out," I yelled. "When are you going to get over yourself? We needed his business."

"We needed him leering at our only daughter less."

The woman was insane if she thought turning away any man that looked sideways at me was good business sense. It wasn't like he'd hit her up to prostitute me out. I pushed through the door, and jumped in the basher. My bare foot jammed down on the accelerator as the car pulled out onto the road, going faster than I probably should have. The tyres squealed with the sharp turn I pulled to make it around the cenotaph. Once on Main Street I slowed, but my head still pounded. How'd she think this was going to wind up? What did she think all those unpaid bills meant? Any business was better than no business, right? At least there would have been some money coming in tonight.

Before I realised where I was going, I'd pulled into my usual park under the ghostly white gum by the stables. I shot out of the old Ford and slammed the door behind me, dust blackening my feet. Jed lifted his head from right where I'd left him this morning, resting in his stall. His huge brown eyes followed my storm along the dusty hall into the tack room, and when I emerged with his bridle he was still watching me. I let myself into his stall and slipped the bit into his mouth and the straps over his ears, then threw the reins up and over his tall head. Being around a horse, with no shoes on was risky. If he stood on my toes they'd snap, but Jed was a gentle giant and I was paying close attention to where both our feet moved. He let me lead him out of the stables and up to the chair that sat out front for just this purpose. Stepping up onto the flat surface, I used it to jump onto Jed's bare back. With no more than a gentle nudge, the giant grey took off, galloping toward the back paddock, while I used my knees against his sides to hold on.

My mother had serious issues. Issues that were costing us money. I probably shouldn't have cared. It wasn't like it was my business. It wasn't like I relied on my parents to pay my college fees. My tuition was accrued through student loans, and government payments paid for my accommodation. My work at Bellevue kept me in a modest allowance, and this time next year I'd be finished and out earning my own keep somewhere the hell away from my mother. If the Akuna went under, then so be it. Still, the idea curdled my stomach. She'd used the proceeds from the sale of Bellevue to fund that damn motel. Throwing away Pop's money with bad business choices made me mad.

The woman even sold her old horse when her father died, and apparently she'd loved riding just as much as I did. Not that I'd ever known her to climb

39

on a horse, so the whole story was a little unbelievable. Who just decided they hated riding one day?

I slid down off my horse and dropped onto the huge rock that had been my pop's favourite fishing spot. Jed nudged my back, as if to remind me he was still there. "Sorry, buddy, I didn't bring any treats."

Crossing my legs schoolkid style, I rested my elbows on my knees and chin in my hands, then gazed out over the creek. The meandering brook was the waterway for which our small town was named, and right here, where it wound its way through the back of Bellevue, the creek was thick, its banks dotted with moss-covered boulders and lined with baby gum trees and native shrubs. Huge willows could be found where the creek ran into the Akuna River, but this little spot was more secluded and so serene the only sound to be heard was the soft bubble of water sliding over the rocky bed.

And a merry whistle.

My head snapped up.

A familiar black hat bopped with the movement of its owner leaping from one huge river rock to another, then to a third, getting closer to my side of the stream. Great. Not sure I was up for another argument, I climbed to my feet and unhooked Jed's reins.

"Leaving already?"

Keeping my eyes on my hands, I mumbled, "Absolutely."

"Hey, Molly ..." Somehow he was now right in front of me, his finger tipping my chin, and forcing eye contact. "I'm up here."

You be careful around him.

Screw you, Mum.

I looked Callan right in the eye; right in his gentle, smoky grey gaze. His teeth caught the corner of his bottom lip, and suddenly the country guy didn't seem so full of himself. His finger fell from my chin, and my breath rushed out. My fingers unclenched to hang loosely at my sides.

"What are you doing here?" I asked.

"I don't know." He blinked those darn deep eyes and something stirred inside me.

"Me neither ..." Although I was beginning to understand that crazy fate Savvy was always talking about. I leaned forward, and Callan's gaze flicked over my shoulder. "Your ride's escaping."

Turning around, I swore at the sight of Jed heading for home.

"Shit." I ran. Something stabbed my foot and I stumbled, but ignoring it, I pushed through the few steps to catch Jed, whose reins must have fallen from my fingers while I was distracted. The cheeky horse thought he could return to the stables without me, the leather reins trailing along the ground with his steady plod. I snatched them up and Jed halted to the sound of a deep chuckle behind us.

It wasn't bloody funny. He could have gotten his leg snagged and fallen. I spun around, glaring at Callan, but my taunt slipped away at his genuine smile. The dappled shade and babbling creek made him seem somehow ...

"Beautiful spot down here." He tilted his chin toward the stream.

I led Jed to an old fallen tree and lifted my foot to survey the damage. No broken skin meant it mustn't have been a sharp stone. "The whole property's gorgeous."

As I stepped up onto the mossy log, Callan tipped the brim of that stupid hat. My blood heated at the smile he dropped, and composing my lust-o-meter with a deep inhale, I jumped onto Jed, heaving myself up to the arch of his back and pulling my leg over his rump. The softness of his coat against my thighs only intensified the feelings the cowboy had stirred up in my lower tummy.

Callan's steady gaze was still on me. "I wish you wouldn't run away all the time."

"I'm not."

Challenging my statement with a continued stare, Callan stepped forward and grabbed the reins next to Jed's mouth. "Then get your pretty arse down off that giant horse and hang around for a bit. You didn't come here just to leave two minutes later."

Pretty arse? Jed tugged against the reins to reach the lush grass by the creek.

"You look like you need to relax."

He was right ... I really wasn't ready to head home and see all those bills. I hoicked a leg over my horse and slid to the ground. Callan's mouth tipped, as if he thought he'd won this battle, and maybe he had. That didn't mean he'd win the war, though.

I secured Jed to his usual tree and sunk onto my rock. Callan took a seat on a smaller one nearby and snapped off a long piece of grass, which he proceeded to twist between his fingers.

"Bellevue's pretty unique." He looked out over the running water. "Bit like you."

Holy hell. I was in cotton shorts and the love-heart T-shirt Savvy hated. Unique wasn't a word my fashion conscious friend would use to describe this look.

Scooting my knees up under my chin, I wrapped my arms around my legs while fiery blood burned my face. Even though my gaze stayed fixed on a dandelion swaying in the slight breeze, I could sense Callan from my periphery, watching, smirking. I swear he made me uncomfortable on purpose.

"So what are you doing with that ... that mountain of tyres in the east paddock?"

He snapped the strand of long grass. "Come to tonight's progress meeting and you'll find out."

I raised a brow, because seriously. "Mysterious much?"

He chuckled. "That's what's keeping you interested."

Rolling my eyes, I pushed off the rock. "I gotta go."

"Come on, I was only joking around. Can't blame me for wanting some company."

I ran my gaze over his trespassing self—this was McLean property darn it—slowing when I reached those thick shoulders. Maybe the progress meeting wouldn't be so bad. It might help me find a way to save the motel.

FIVE

I fidgeted in the hard plastic seat, my hands balled in my lap while beside me, Dad watched Tessa Gibson intently. He'd been to a few Progress Committee meetings before, so when I told him about the one tonight he was happy to come along. Honestly, attending a meeting probably wasn't a bad idea. At least then we'd know where the Akuna stood in the grand scheme of things. If there'd be enough tourists coming to town to keep our little motel running. If there were ... then how we could go about promoting our business. And if there weren't ... then how we could help pull more people into town.

After giving the minutes of the last meeting, Tessa asked if anyone wanted to take the floor. I glanced around the hall, blinking when the setting sun caught my eye through the high window.

"The mud run is all set to go," Marshall's voice carried through the timber-floored hall. I spun around and spotted him standing a few rows back, Callan lounging in the chair beside him, sans hat. The cowboy's dark hair looked almost black and although not long, it curled a little near his temples. "Cal here has helped with a strong advertising campaign, not just hitting up the newspapers of our neighbouring towns, but spreading the word through social media. We've got the entire event just about covered, and ticket sales are close to outstripping expenses. We're hoping to sell a whole lot more. With luck ..." he scratched the back of his neck, "we'll draw in more outsiders from nearby towns."

Movement drew my attention to Callie-May, sitting prim and proper in a pale pink button shirt so fitted it showed off the exact shape of her chest.

"Sounds great," Tessa said.

People from out of town ... I raised a hand and Marshall nodded for me to speak. "Where are all these out-of-towners staying? Could we ..." I glanced at my dad, who raised a go-ahead brow, "... offer an accommodation-with-entry special deal?"

"Great idea, Molly." Marshall nodded. "Why don't you talk to your people about that and come to me with a room fee, then we'll throw it into our latest adverts?"

"When's it happening?"

"In two weeks."

Pinching my bottom lip between my teeth, I dropped into my seat to meet Dad's look of approval. "Nice work."

Having delivered all the requisite information, Marshall returned to his seat and Tessa looked around the hall again for her next speaker. A mud run sounded like fun, but in the dry east paddock of Bellevue surely it wouldn't be possible to make a decent course. The creek ran through the rear of Marshall's land, but it wasn't thick and easily accessible like the waterway was in my paddock.

Dan Molyneaux gave an update on the Riverview Hotel, skimming through the details of the Bushman's Ball I'd seen advertised the other day. Things in our little town were moving forward, which was great. It turned out that there was even more competition for the Akuna Motel than I'd first thought; apparently Stevie Ryan had cleaned up the old cottage on her property and was offering it up for short-term stays. Then of course the buzz about the Figtree Lodge tickled the room more than once. Everyone had high hopes for Bindarra Creek, and I couldn't help but feel just as positive as the rest of the townsfolk.

Finally, the meeting wrapped up and Dad moseyed over to the kitchen where someone had set up a hot urn and a plate of cakes. Trust him to track down the food.

"Hey there."

I spun around to meet Callan's lazy smile. Cropped close to his head, his dark hair matched the slight shadow of stubble across his jaw, and somehow made those grey eyes seem even deeper.

"H ... hi."

"It's so soft," I murmured, gliding my hands over a shaved head. "Not spiky at all."

"Mmm." He kissed the corner of my mouth, then placed another tender kiss on the centre of it. After that, nothing sweet or innocent marked the way he kissed me, or the way I kissed him back, and all thoughts of hair fell away as we lost ourselves to the moment. Our bodies moved to the thump of the music in

the distance.

"Molly ..." Callan's smile had gone, replaced by a frown. "You're running away again."

Heat flushed my neck, rushing to my cheeks. "Sorry ... I was just ..."

Why was I thinking about this now? He raised a dark brow, but it seemed I'd once again lost all ability to speak. Callan's head dipped to the side as if he were waiting for me to say something.

"Ah ... I ... what ..." I dropped my gaze to my toes. Frig, I couldn't even think straight.

"About the room deals, what did you have in mind?"

I blew out a shaky breath and pulled myself together. He was just a guy. A really hot guy.

"Right. Umm ... we could use the extra business, so I think if we set the room rate a bit above cost, maybe that will help draw people in and also make us a little profit. I ah ... I have to run it by management first though."

He nodded. "Sounds good."

His finger smoothed the flesh between my brows. "Whatever is causing this, it's not worth worrying over."

I should have stepped away, placing him firmly out of my space, but for some unknown reason my feet were stuck.

He offered up another smile and sauntered toward the table of cakes. Hot damn, the guy could move, all lazy and smooth and—

He looked back.

"And Molly ..." He closed the distance between us, dropping his voice to a husky whisper. "You should compete in the mud run. Getting down and dirty again might be fun." His mouth eased into another lazy smile, and he winked.

Again?

"Molly?" Head spinning, I turned my attention to the woman who had chaired the meeting and now stood beside my dad. "I don't believe we've met."

"Hi." I offered my hand. "It's nice to meet you."

"Likewise."

Again. Did he really say that?

I smiled at Tessa. "So, you're the lady responsible for all the changes around town."

"Not exactly," she said. "I just got the ball rolling."

"Excuse me, Tessa." The mayor drew our host's attention away. "Pastor Miller wanted to speak to you about possible funding for restoration of the church windows."

She nodded, and took a step away. "Excuse me, Molly."

The moment Tessa was gone, I turned to Dad. "They give out funding grants here?"

He sipped on his tea. "Well, yes, sometimes, but the circumstances need to be—"

"So, you're telling me they might help with the Akuna?"

Money was what we needed in order to generate more money. Maybe this progress committee was just the thing to save our little motel.

He cringed. "It's not likely. They mostly raise money for things that improve the town overall, not individual businesses."

An overloud giggle drew my attention to the table of cakes where Callie-May stood with her knee bent and foot balancing on her toes like a horse resting a lazy leg. A stupidly giggling horse, tossing its blonde mane around as if on show for the Akubra-less cowboy pouring himself a coffee from the urn.

"Hmm. A mud run ..." Dad twisted his tea cup around.

"It's a great idea, but the east paddock will be ruined."

"I'm sure it won't be that bad, honey. Everything will grow back, and they'll make sure there aren't any hazards left behind for the horses."

"I just hate seeing the farm changed ..."

"I know."

It was probably overly sentimental of me, but every change that had happened in the past few years made me feel that little more further removed from Pop. Dad was right, though. This one wasn't a big deal.

Callie-May caught my gaze as she sauntered past us.

"You're right," I said to Dad. "A mud run's no biggie. It's not like they're making any major changes."

But then there had been that Bindarra Building Company man in the suit.

SIX

Sliding the shovel under a pile of day-old manure, I balanced the full load while pinning my phone between my shoulder and ear. "A mud run. You know, like a fun run, but through an obstacle course of ditches and trenches and rope climb thingies covering troughs of water ..."

"Liv's the sporty one. Maybe you should ask her."

"You'd love it, Savvy."

Angel brayed. Jed nudged my back and the phone slipped from my grip to drop against the dirty straw. Muttering under my breath, I dumped the shovel on the ground and picked up my fumbled mobile.

"Sorry about that."

"Where are you?" Savvy asked.

"Mucking out stables."

She made a disgusted noise. "Now that's the perfect place to wear your horrible Hello Kitty shirt."

"Hey! I happen to love that shirt." I glanced down at the cute white kitten gracing the front of my pink

T-shirt, wondering how the hell she knew I had it on. "So are you coming? There'll be half-naked hot guys ... or you could just bring Dane. Imagine him smeared in mud."

"That sounds like fun, but I'm not sure Dane's up to it. He's been pretty down since his dad ..." She didn't need to finish the sentence. *Since his dad passed away.*

"Maybe it's just what he needs."

"Dane," she shouted down the line. I pulled the phone away from my ear. "Wanna take me to visit Molly? There's mud wrestling involved. And horses. I think I can hear horses."

"You can," I said. "And speaking of horses, I need to get back to work."

"Definitely horses." Silence stretched between our phones, then Savvy returned. "I think we're good to go. I'll get back to you, though; things change every day at the moment."

"Awesome. Miss you, Sav."

"I miss you too. Talk soon."

"Of course."

"Mwah."

The line went dead, so I shoved the phone back in my jeans pocket and resumed mucking out Jed's stall. With a full shovel, I turned for the door, and *shit.* I jumped, sending manure flying in all directions. One piece almost clocked Callan where he leaned, arms on the top rail of the door, watching me work. My heart must have bypassed at least a few beats, before I blew out a long breath and sucked in one to replace it, all while he watched me, grin in place.

"A flip phone?"

"Not everyone needs to access Facebook twenty-four/seven." *Or has the money for a smart phone.* I pushed the shovel under a pile of dung.

He tapped his index finger on the rail. "Talked to your folks about that room rate?"

"One hundred and twenty dollars a night, twin share."

He nodded as if he thought that was a fair deal. "Any restrictions?"

"Umm ..." We hadn't thought about that. "Nope. 'Scuse me." I pointedly looked at the full shovel, its weight growing heavy in my arms. Still leaning on the aged timber, Callan dropped a hand over the side and released the latch, then swung the door open. I shuffled through, and his hands dropped onto the shovel handle just above mine. "Where's this going?"

"I've got it." I didn't let go.

He raised a brow and gently pulled the tool toward himself.

"Fine." I sighed. "Into the half-full chaff bag out there."

Smiling that ridiculous smile that I just knew was grounded in self-satisfaction, he hefted the load up and walked it to the white bag. Dumping the horse dung inside, he then planted the shovel in the hard dirt floor and leaned against it. "Want to see my course?"

Heat sprung into my cheeks.

"Molly." The stupid grin returned. "I just want to show you my course. You can tell me how hard it is."

The guy was so damn full of himself, but I was kind of curious about how he was going to pull off a mud run out here. It wasn't like Bindarra had an impending wet season.

I offered up a small smile and he led me out of the

stables. Together, we walked toward the east paddock. Even from here, I could see a fresh mound of dirt that hadn't been there yesterday. How I missed that on my trek up the long drive, I couldn't be sure. "How long's the course?"

He glanced across at me, and his lip twitched. For the love of God ... "I meant how hard?" His mouth flicked right up and his eyes glittered. "Difficult ... how damn difficult is the darn thing?"

Callan burst out laughing. Once he'd gotten over himself, he said, "Nothing like the huge mud runs they do in the city. This is more about tricky obstacles and less about distance covered."

"Won't it churn up the paddock? What are you going to do with the horses?"

"Being stabled for a few days won't hurt them."

We reached the gate and I unlatched it, swinging the iron structure wide enough for us both to pass though. I latched it behind us and Callan inclined his head toward a long trench. "That's the starting point."

Old wire gates covered the top of the trench, preventing anyone from getting in or out. "Commando crawling though that when it's half full of muddy water, then climbing out the other end and scaling the tyre climb—"

"Wait. Where's all the water coming from? This dirt is rock hard." I stamped a foot against the ground.

"Ah." Callan tapped his nose. "I've got that covered."

"You can't possibly have a permit to pump from the creek for this, and any water is going to soak right into the ground anyway ..." I trailed off, considering all the options. We might have had a little rain lately, but Bindarra Creek still wasn't lush. It took a long while to come back from dusty drought-stricken land to something worthy of mud. I'd seen it happen once before.

Although ... the morning after the B&S I'd slip in mud when I was making a mad dash for the basher, and all that mess had been caused from a water fight.

I willed myself to remember last September. Nothing came. Not a flash of a steamy kiss, nor the heat of a sure hand. Some way to lose one's virginity.

"What do you think?"

"It's umm ..." I eyed up the roped off ditches, and farther away, a dirt pile steep enough to make weary legs ache. "You sure made a mess of the paddock."

"Yeah." He smiled. "Seize the day."

"How does that make any sense?"

He shook his head and the way he looked at me made the hairs on the back of my neck rise with a whole-body shiver. He reached up, his finger brushing the underside of my chin. "Just live for the moment, baby. That's all that matters."

Swallowing the sudden flood in my mouth, I held his steady gaze.

"I do." Well, I did at least once. I gave him my most confident smile then turned back toward the stables. I had a head full of sketchy memories to prove being impulsive wasn't always the wisest choice.

****

Room ten's orange door stood open. Mum was on the front desk which meant the cheery whistle coming out of the guest room had to be Dad. Not that Mum would have been whistling anyway. Now in cool cotton shorts and a tank, I took a swig out of my bottle of water as I walked along the flaking path. Upon reaching the entry, I took in the ugly yellow paint that my parents had never updated. The bed's stripped-off cover lay in a heap on the floor while Dad smoothed out a fresh, more modern plain grey piece.

"Nice." I walked into the room. "Where'd you score this?"

"It's from a liquidation sale. Pre-used. It's nice though, huh?"

"It looks great, Dad. So much better than that flowery thing." I waved toward the faded brown floral bedspread crumpled in the corner. A new lamp sat on the rickety bedside table. With a silver shade and chrome base, it matched the doona nicely.

"Did you speak to the committee about a grant?" That had to be where the money came from.

"Yes, and they don't issue funds to individual establishments. We've got to do this on our own, Mols."

"Maybe we could organise a fu ..." The words died on my lips. With all the other fundraisers happening in town and me only home for a few months, there was no way we could pull something together.

"It looks great," I said, backing out of the room.

I jumped in the basher, even though it went against my only-to-work policy, and cranked up the radio. Taylor Swift's latest hit filled the car amid crackling static, and I reached around to twist the wire coat hanger acting as an antenna. A few moments of work and the signal cleared up.

It was only a two-minute drive to reach our local

hardware store, but I couldn't have walked with what I had planned. Gritting my teeth at who I was about to see, I ducked inside, and Callie-May approached me right away.

I put on my best fake smile for her. "I'm after a tin of paint."

"Finally doing something about the ugly place you call home, huh?" She smiled and turned to lead me to the product I'd requested. "Indoor or outdoor? Gloss or matt?"

"Ah ..." I floundered. "Indoor and matt, I guess. I'm after a neutral colour, maybe white, or something that will look good with grey."

"Easy." She plucked a tin off the shelf then turned back to me. "What size were you after?"

The price tag for the one in her hand read $63.69. The next size up was almost a hundred dollars. "How far will that one go?"

"Should cover a standard-sized room with a ton left over, or you know, the vomit green walls in a motel's reception."

"That'll do."

It wasn't worth biting at her stupid insults, so I waited in silence while she mixed the colour, then I paid for the can and a roller and placed it in the back of the basher before heading home. When I swung into the parking lot, the door to room ten was still open, so I hefted the heavy tin out of the backseat and tapped the car door closed with my foot. Still hard at work, Dad was fighting with a sea of lace curtains as they tumbled to the floor around him. The drapes already sat in a pile by the door.

I set the can on the faded laminate of the writing desk and placed the roller beside it. Dad looked at me square on, shrewd-eyed. "I told you not to waste your college funds."

"Then consider it a Christmas gift."

It was official. Room ten would soon be made over.

SEVEN

Peering around the money-Christmas-tree hybrid and over my mother's shoulder at the booking sheet, I was pleasantly surprised to see all the red squares centred around December fifteen. Whatever online promotion Callan had done was working. We weren't full, but there were certainly more bookings than on any other day this month, or than there had been a week ago. With room ten looking fabulous and ready for guests, next week was sure to rake in some profits.

"Can you watch the desk for a few minutes? I need to duck out."

"Sure can." I slid into the seat she'd vacated, and my mother scooped up her purse. "Where are you going?"

"Just down the street for a bit. I need to take care of a few things."

She fled through the madly-dinging door and I flicked a quick text to Joy to let her know I was coming in later than usual, then turned to the tinsel-trimmed computer. It'd been weeks since I'd managed to check social media, and it looked like not much had changed in my absence. Savvy had filled the stream with pics of the beach and her boyfriend surfing, while Liv was a little quieter. There was just the odd update about loving work at the sports centre or the delicious meal she'd last cooked for 'her boys'. Both my best friends were serenely happy. They made relationships look so easy. Logan grounded Liv, and Dane had a way of keeping Savvy real. Perfect matches like my friends enjoyed weren't hard to come by—they were near impossible.

I clicked the link to invite friends to the mud run, making sure to include Liv and Savvy, their boyfriends, and Logan's brother.

The front doorbell jingled and I looked up, expecting to see Mum returning, but John Smithfield walked in the door. A rep for some farming equipment company, he often passed through town on business. He took a candy cane from the bowl on the counter. "Haven't seen you in a while."

"I've been at college for the past few months."

"Good for you. What are you studying?"

"Vet Science."

Unwrapping the candy, he whistled. "You've got the smarts then."

Blushing, I ducked my head and picked up a pen. Swirling it around the booking sheet, I said, "It's hard work, but I'm almost done. Are you checking out?"

"I am. That new room sure is something. Nice change."

"Thanks." I grinned up at him. "You nearly missed out; we've only just opened that one back up."

The bell rattled again, and John turned over his

shoulder just as Mum entered. "Patricia, I was telling your girl here how much I like the new look."

Mum looked from me to our guest as if she thought I'd put him up to dishing out praise. "Thanks, John. I'm glad you had a good stay."

"Make sure you put me down for room ten whenever I'm in town."

"Will do." Mum smiled, while I rung up his account.

"Just the room, John? Did you have anything from the mini bar?"

"Not this time, darlin'."

"If you can sign this, please ..." I tapped the signature line with my pen, "... we'll bill it back to your company."

"Perfect." He winked at me. "Good luck with the study." John reached for the door and pulled it open. "I'll see you next time, ladies."

"Bye." I pushed myself up off the stool and moved out of the way for my mother to take over. She sighed, then dumped her bag under the counter.

Leaving my mother to stew over John's words, I ducked upstairs and grabbed my bag. With it slung over my shoulder, I retreated to the basher only to get side-tracked by the sweep of a straw broom hitting stone. The patch of driveway Dad had already cleaned stood out against the dirty grey concrete. He didn't see me coming, so when I tapped on his shoulder he near jumped out of his skin. Laughing, Dad leaned on the broom.

"Off to Bellevue?"

"Yeah. I thought you'd like to know that work we did on room ten paid off. John Smithfield just checked out and said he wants that room whenever he stays."

Dad shook his head with a smile. "Nice work, Molly. You were on the money with suggesting a makeover."

"Yeah ..." I tightened my ponytail. "We just need to figure out how to finance doing a few more rooms."

"I've been thinking about that." He gave the driveway an idle sweep. "I might visit the bank. There are a few cheaper alternatives, like ex-stock clearances, but it's going to be a slow process. We could need to do one room at a time and start with the little things."

My phone buzzed in my bag, reminding me I was running later by the moment. "I'll put some thought into it." I backed away. "Later, Dad."

"See ya, sweetie." He took up sweeping again and walking away, I fished out my phone. Olivia's name filled the screen.

We're in. Tell me all the details so we can both get off work.

Smiling, I flicked back:

You're coming! It should be loads of fun and I can't wait to see you.
Dec 15th, 9.30a.m. start. Not your average mud run; it's more of a 'dust run'.
You guys can stay at my place if you want.

I climbed in the old paddock basher and steered her out of the parking lot.

No less than ten minutes later, the huge white homestead at Bellevue crowded my rear-vision mirror as I pulled up at the stables. The east paddock looked like a plastic-covered hot mess. Synthetic yellow sheets lined the long ditch and waving his arms about, Callan directed some kind of small dozer. Wooden stakes stuck out of the ground, marking the course. With only a few days to go, things were starting to shape up.

Reaching to the passenger seat to grab my bag, I hopped out of the car and moseyed into the stables. The scent of musty straw overpowered every other smell, but still, I drew in a long breath.

Something didn't quite feel right. The place was too quiet, or maybe the air was too cool. I couldn't be sure. Squinting against the unwelcome mid-morning sun, I surveyed my stables. Jed was where I'd left him. Angel's stall stood empty. The mountain pony was also gone. In fact, my gentle giant was the only horse here. That wasn't what made the place feel wrong though. There was something else ... Tilting my head to the side, I took another step forward. A *thunk* echoed my step, then another.

Walking right past the tack room, I pushed open the door of the never-used office. Marshall sat behind my pop's desk, a box on the top of it and a pile of papers in his hand. Surprise could have blown me over. No one ever used this dusty old room that had once been the hub of Pop's business. Marshall preferred to take care of all the things in his office at the house.

"Umm, hi." I dumped my bag in the corner, my gaze rising to the row of old horseshoes lining the wall. Brandy, Missy, Blaze, Storm ... they'd all lived here at one time or another.

Marshall looked up just as he reached for another pile of dusty files lining the back wall. He hefted an armful onto the table. "G'day, Molly."

Examining the top piece of paper, he set it aside and moved on to the next one. The discarded papers he placed into one of several boxes sitting by the desk. Each one held a varied sized stack of yellowed documents. My pop's handwriting was scrawled across everything, so all the paperwork must have been from times long gone. A noticeboard hung on the back wall, pictures of horses and their people all over it. The one that stood out though, was a picture of Jed's huge head hovering over ten-year-old me as I cuddled into my pop's side. Marshall had offered it to me once, but I liked it up there where Pop had pinned it.

He dropped a handful of files onto the desk, its *thunk* billowing dust into the air and I asked, "Where are all the ponies?"

"Cal moved 'em."

"Why?"

"Something about making space."

"For what? They aren't *gone*, gone. Are they?"

Distracted, Marshall still hadn't looked up. "Why don't you ask Cal?"

"Alrighty." I backed out of the room and let myself into Jed's stall. The big grey's head hung low, and his eyes were closed. His tail gave the odd flick to shoo away pesky flies, even as he dozed.

I went about mucking out all the stalls and refreshed Jed's water. Afterward, I gave him a biscuit of hay then trudged over to the east paddock in search of the horse-napper. The little bulldozer now rested in a corner, its driver nowhere in sight, while Callan worked in the ditch, using a shovel to spread out a huge pile of black dirt.

He flashed that slow smile when he noticed me standing on the chicken wire gate that had covered the hole the last time I was here.

"Why don't you just run the course through the creek? That'd have to be easier than all this lining."

"And upset the fragile ecosystem?"

I snorted. I didn't mean to; the laugh had caught me by surprise. "Like this isn't turning the entire farm on its head."

Callan continued pushing around the dirt before looking up at me with that stupidly sexy smile again. "Ah, but grasshoppers and field mice aren't quite so delicate as tadpoles and platypi."

Was he making fun of me? I couldn't quite be sure. Frowning, I kicked at the wire gate. "What'd you do with my ponies?"

"*Your* ponies?" The shovel stopped and he raised a cocky brow.

I held my ground with a raised brow of my own. Take that, Mr Schmooze. I was getting better at handling him. "Angel, Flash, the young filly ..."

"Oh, *those* ponies." He resumed moving dirt. "I popped them in the back paddock for a bit."

"What? That paddock isn't for public access, and it isn't part of Bellevue." *Anymore, thanks to Mum.* "Why can't they stay in the stables while the mud run's happening?"

Callan dropped the shovel and planted a hand on the side of the ditch, then used it to hoist himself up and out of the trench. Landing beside me, he didn't even bother pulling himself up to full height, but rather slouched, bringing us eye to eye. "Who's the boss around here?"

He had me there. Technically it was Marshall, not me. I floundered for a few seconds, while my tongue tried to tie itself into a knot. My fingers twisted around themselves and looking at them, I mumbled, "True."

"Hey." His finger brushed the underside of my chin in what seemed to be a newly formed habit. "You want those horses in the stables, I'll put them back as soon as the mud run's over."

My heart did this stupid thing where it felt like it ran back flips, and I forced myself to meet his gaze. Callan's eyes were like liquid pools of grey, their depth never-ending. The back of his fingers brushed my cheek, and my heart did that crazy thing again. The next breath I drew shook.

Callan stepped closer, and my heart beat faster while his eyes bore into my soul.

His finger grazed my lips, and oh no, what was I doing?

I stepped back and back again, then spun around, but the chicken wire foiled my speedy retreat, my foot catching in the gate. I tripped. My butt hit the ground and oh my lord, the embarrassment. Heat flooded my face, my chest too, as I scrambled to get vertical, but my damn foot just wouldn't come free.

Callan dropped to his haunches and gentle fingers pushed my tattered Doc out of the twisted wire. I took an unsteady breath and he stood, extending his hand. I looked at it like a stupid person for a good few moments, until a slow smile crept over his strong features. Geez, I was so clueless sometimes. I placed my hand in his, and Callan pulled me to my feet. A mumbled "thank you" passed my lips, and this time I stepped away more carefully. Still facing him, I took another step and another, until I finally turned and walked full speed toward the stables.

His shouted words followed my retreat. "You're running away again."

EIGHT

"Lone Wolf McLean ..."

My tummy clenched at the voice spawned right out of hell, and I raised my gaze from my feet and into the shrewd eyes of my high school tormentor. Dressed in a shiny red number that glittered with each new breath, Callie-May looked as stunning as ever. Fake, too. Her white-blonde hair was twisted up into some kind of fancy bun, and so much makeup coated her face she'd probably used a bricklayer's trowel to slather it on.

"Callie-May." I smiled.

Her gaze slipped to my borrowed flat shoes then examined every inch of me all the way to my braided hair, lingering on my grandma's cameo necklace. "I see nothing's changed with you. Still a loser."

"And I see you're still a cow."

Coming here had been a stupid idea. I shouldn't have bothered. Should have known it wouldn't have been just out-of-towners when a few of my ex-classmates had never left Bindarra.

"Still a friendless loner."

"Get stuffed, Callie-May. You know nothing about me."

"I know your chances of picking up an eligible bachelor tonight are ... umm ... let me see ... non-existent."

"The eligible bachelors can bite my arse and so can you, because that's not what these balls are about."

She glanced toward her friend and they both laughed. "I thought nerds were supposed to be smart. What do you think B&S stands for?"

"Bull and shit."

A heavy arm fell around my shoulders. The spicy masculine cologne tickled my senses as a gravelly voice said, "There you are, baby. I've been looking all over for you."

Stubble grazed my chin as a pair of tender lips landed on my own. Strong fingers glided up my spine and tangled in the hair at the back of my neck. He smiled against my mouth, and his tongue skated over the seam of my lips.

My heart flipped, my tummy dipped, and my head skipped.

The stranger broke our kiss, turning side on and tugging me into the space against his hip as he shifted his attention to Callie-May. "Sorry ... ah ..."

Frowning, she snapped her gaping mouth closed. "You know exactly who I am."

****

The *no vacancy* sign shone out front like a bright red beacon of hope. Hope that we could manage to pull off more nights like the last. The car park had spilled over yesterday evening and every bed had a body or two in it. I guess people didn't want to drive all the way out to Bindarra Creek in the early morning to hit the mud challenge straight away. They'd rather face the course fresh, not travel weary.

The bell chimed again and this time my friend Liv

walked through. With expensive-looking runners, gym pants and a baggy white T-shirt, she sure looked the part. Pity it was all going to get trashed, especially those pretty shoes.

"I hope you don't love those runners."

She glanced at the colourful shoes, shrugged, then raised her gaze to my mum. Liv offered up a cheery smile and my mother gave my friend a onceover in return. Liv didn't seem to notice; she just continued smiling. "I've come to steal Molly away for the day. I hope you can survive without her."

Mum made herself busy with the booking sheet. "I'm sure we'll manage."

Liv kicked the smile up a notch higher. "It was so nice to meet you, Mrs McLean."

Looking past my uber-pleasant friend and out the glass door, Mum frowned. "You too, Olivia. Have fun today."

With a hand on her shoulder, I spun Liv around and pushed her toward the door. Outside, her boyfriend, Logan, had propped himself against the passenger side of his red Corolla, his blond waves twisted into a low ponytail. When we emerged, he opened the car door.

"Ready?"

"Yes," Liv chirped. "Let's go get dirty."

Logan chuckled and another head appeared out of the back window. "Hot damn, Livie, you can't go saying shit like that in public."

Logan clipped his brother upside the back of his head, and Jordan punched Logan's arm then slid across to the other side of the back seat. Liv was already in, so I got in the back with Jordan.

"How'd you sleep, J?"

"Not bad, Miss Molly." He snapped in his belt. "It should be a great day. Did you see those babes in room ten? If they're rolling in the mud with us, then I'm in heaven."

Logan eyeballed his younger brother in the rearview mirror. "Show some respect, Jordan. Women aren't meat."

"What the hell, bro? It was only a few months ago that you would've been right there beside me, fighting for the one with the biggest tits."

Liv shook her head, and Jordan tossed me a wink, mouthing, *"Wait for it ..."*

He chuckled, and I couldn't help but smile back. I'd even missed this bratty high-schooler over the past few weeks. Although Bindarra was home, it wasn't the sanctuary it once had been. Lately, worry overrode the relaxed feeling Bellevue had always created in me. Even though Mum had sold the property, I loved the way Marshall and Joy had preserved Pop's land. But now when the land that should have one day been mine was at risk of dire change, being there didn't bring the joy it once had. Not like the creek still did, and not like the joy I was feeling by being reunited with my friends. Maybe, just maybe, home was more than a place.

Jordan slumped back in the seat. The car spluttered a few times before turning over and Logan let it idle for a moment while Liv looked at me over her shoulder. "How's break been? The motel sure seems busy."

"Busy for one night. It's actually been really dead."

She frowned. "Oh."

"Yeah. It's not good."

Logan inched the car back out of its space and Liv

turned around, moving her hand to cover Logan's on the shift.

"What about you guys?" I asked. "Have you seen anyone?"

"Nope." Logan swung out onto Mount Ingalls Road. "We're the only ones crazy enough to hang around during summer break."

"I swear the town loses half its population when classes aren't on," Liv said. "Even the sports centre's quiet. Pity Savvy and Dane couldn't make it. With his dad—"

"What the fuck is that?" Jordan peered out his side widow, leaning against the glass and looked up as we went around the cenotaph.

"Jordan!" Logan's glare pinned his brother through the mirror again. "Keep it clean."

A laugh burst out of the younger Hays, filling the car with its gusto.

"It's a war memorial." I shuddered.

"Why the hell did they put it in the centre of the goddamn road?"

Logan shook his head. "You're in the country, bro."

"Take a right here," I ordered without looking up at the imposing soldier standing to attention, hands resting on the butt of his rifle. There was something about that thing which gave me the heebie jeebies.

We reached the turn onto Bindarra Creek Road, and Bellevue was still at least a kilometre away, but we slowed to a steady crawl. Good old BC had never seen this much traffic. It took a good fifteen minutes to cover the distance that usually spanned less than five. As we drove over Swallow's Bridge with Bellevue in sight, I realised just the extent of this event. Cars lined the side of the road. Tape cordoned off the edges of Bellevue's driveway, no doubt to prevent people parking along the dirt track. Marshall stood at the grid directing traffic up toward the stables, where rows of cars had parked. It was a pretty impressive turnout.

"Pop the window down," I told Jordan and using the winder, he followed my request. I leaned across him. "Morning, Marshall. Do you need any help? It looks busy."

"Molly." He glanced toward the stables, then over to the east paddock. "Callan's got plenty of help on the course; maybe check in with Joy at the canteen."

"No worries." I nodded, and Logan rolled away from the main gates.

Liv turned around to look at me. "I thought you weren't working today."

"Technically I'm not. They might need an extra set of hands though."

People filled the east paddock, all wearing numbered bibs on their backs. The crowd seemed at its thickest around one end of the longest trench Callan had worked so tirelessly on. The town's water hauler had backed up to the trench and the rural fire service truck was parked across the field. Both water carriers helped to create plenty of mud. It was an epic waste of water, but the mud run had brought life back into the town. Besides, Marshall had said the event more than paid for itself.

We drove right up to the stables and parked with the other cars. We all piled out and Jordan whistled. "That's friggin' epic."

"Sure looks like fun." Liv reached for her boyfriend's hand. "Why's no one on the course yet?

They're not starting us all at once like a race, are they?"

"I don't think so ..." Standing on my tiptoes I peered into the stables, but a small group of people blocked my view of where Joy should be set up. "I'm gonna have to leave you guys for a bit and see if they need any help."

Liv nodded, and I slipped through the people to find Joy working inside one of the empty stables. Sitting behind a desk placed at the open gate, she had a bunch of bibs in a box beside her and a long list of names spread out over the table. The majority of them were highlighted in bright pink. She handed over two bibs to the girl in front of the desk then looked up at the next person in line. "Hi there."

"Hello," the middle-aged man said. "I'm registering for Adamson."

Joy skimmed the pen down the page until she found his name. "Two adults and two juniors?"

"That's the one."

She counted out four bibs. "The kids are both over eight?"

"Yep."

"And you're aware they must be accompanied by a guardian throughout the course?"

"Not a problem."

Joy smiled as she passed him the numbers. "The course starts over by the water tanker. Enjoy your day, Mr Adamson."

The man shuffled off and Joy turned her attention to me. "Hi Molly. Just take the number of bibs you need, and I'll cross you off the list."

"I thought you might need some help."

"Oh." She looked up at me. "That would be

wonderful. The boxes of food and drink back there need to be set up for after the run."

"On it."

I ran the bibs out to my friends then returned, turning to the piles of Eskies and food. A stack of posters sat on the nearest box, advertising what we had. Marshall and Callan hadn't missed any opportunities to rake in a few extra dollars. I worked away, making displays and sticking up price signs along the stable walls. To make things easier for Joy later, I shuffled drinks around in the giant Eskies so one was filled with sports drinks and water, while the other was chock full of soft drinks. People must have started buying as they registered, because Joy took to calling out orders and I wound up passing them to her almost as quickly as I set displays up. Then it seemed all of a sudden, things died down.

"Molly, dear, why don't you go join your friends? I'll be alright here now."

I realigned the stack of barbeque chips, which were in peril of toppling over. "You're sure?"

"Go. Have fun!"

"Okay."

As I picked up the bib I'd set aside earlier, and pinned it onto my T-shirt, Joy's hand cupped my shoulder. "And Molly ..."

"Yes?"

"Thanks for your help. You truly are a godsend."

"I'm sorry I wasn't here earlier."

She made a shooing motion. "Off with you."

I backed out of the stall that hadn't housed a horse in a few years and scanned the activity in the east paddock as I made my way across to the starting line. Callan must have opened the course while I was helping, as it swarmed with people, yet it seemed that no one was quite finished yet. Dirty bodies crowded all the tyre climbs and the trenches teemed with laughing runners. Finding Liv and Logan wouldn't be easy. Finding Callan, though? Simple.

With that black hat shading his eyes, Callan stood by the huge cylindrical tank of the water hauler. Dressed in fitted jeans, and a country-style checked button-down, he sure didn't look as if he intended to hit the muddy course.

As I came through the propped open gate my foot caught on a rock and I stumbled.

"Molly!" Jordan's shout cut through the ruckus that was one hundred-plus people laughing and squealing as they ran, fell, and flung mud. Covered in reddish brown gunk, he met me halfway across the field with a full-body hug. It wasn't like I intended to keep my blue T-shirt in its pristine state, so throwing my arms around his shoulders, I let him smear his dirty clothes all over me and even used my fingers to squeeze some grossness out of the bottom of his shirt.

"No squealing? You're no fun," Jordan complained.

I smeared the gunk across his cheek.

Grinning, Jordan said, "But at least you're finally free. Let's hit this thing."

I glanced across at Callan, who was now busy talking to a group of locals—a few of the Sullivans and a bunch of other townsfolk, by the look of it.

I mustn't have been moving fast enough for my energetic friend, because he tugged on my arm, pulling me toward the course. "Come on already. I've had enough of playing third wheel to the Logan and

Olivia show, so let's do this."

Laughing, I pulled away. "You can't escape being their third wheel, mate. You live with them."

"Loser buys lunch." Jordan took off, racing toward the tyre climb which he scaled with an ungodly ease. By the time I'd reached the base and started heaving myself up the rubber ladder, Jordan had already hit the top. Balancing rather well, he leaned over the edge and shouted, "And the king wins!"

"King schming." Using my arms to pull myself up onto the next rung, then the next, I concentrated on making the peak. "Just 'cause you're a footy jock—"

"Footy has nothing to do with my climbing prowess."

I let go with one hand, and making a fist, flexed my arms. "Your guns, J. Your guns."

He let out an almighty belly roar and I heaved myself onto the top of the stupidly high tower, only when I looked down, the ground wasn't that far below at all. The tower was probably only a little taller than my full height. I took a moment to catch my breath. Callan still stood over by the water cooler, and was still surrounded by a host of locals. He lifted a hand and waved. All the people turned around and so did I, but there was only air behind us. Certainly not anyone waving back at him.

Except Jordan. I glanced at my young friend then back at Callan, who lifted his hat and dipped his chin.

Jordan grinned from ear to ear. "Who's that waving at you?"

"No one."

"No one?" He chuckled. "Yeah, right."

Then he slid down the tyre climb faster than he'd

scaled it, leaving me at the top, still watching Callan watching our race.

"Sure hope you're loaded, 'cause I'm gonna be half starved after this."

Jordan took off across the dusty ground, covering the distance between the tyre climb and the muddy trench like it was nothing. Meanwhile, I finally pulled myself together enough to drag my attention back to our race. Dropping down the other side of the tyre tower, I let my feet guide me to the ground then chased after the rugby player who could outrun just about anyone on the field. How this race was fair, I'd never know.

I hit the earth running, my feet pounding the hard dirt, and by the time I'd reached the next obstacle— one of those side-by-side tyre lines where you put a foot in each circle as you run through it—Jordan had stopped at the far end to let me catch up. I guess he wasn't such a torment after all. Or maybe he was, because no sooner than I'd jumped through the rubbery maze, he reached out and tapped my shoulder.

"You haven't won yet."

He dove into the shallow water of a fake creek, his stomach probably scraping along the muddy base. As soon as his sliding momentum slowed, he scrambled to his feet and ran through the fake waterway, making an almighty splash. He made good ground until one of the firies noticed his mad dash and hit him with the hose. I laughed my arse off when he fell into the muddy water. Jordan struggled to his feet, but the water blasted him back down again. My side ached, and clutching it, I kept laughing. With the wide hose propped on his hip, the firefighter, whose name I should have remembered, yelled, "Go, Molly."

I entered the man-made creek with far less show. My feet sank into the knee-deep mud, and lifting them proved far harder than expected. The weight of the water slowed me down. The fire hose never came my way, thank goodness, because I struggled enough to stay upright without that added complication.

Jordan finally managed to get a foothold and wasted no time in surging ahead.

Who knew what I'd be able to buy him for lunch? He wouldn't want pizza, since he worked with it all the time. I hated Chinese ... so maybe a burger and chips from Beth's. That truck stop made the best hamburgers in the entire New England region.

My foot slipped.

My shoe twisted.

Fire shot through my arch up my ankle, and I fell into the watery ditch. My hands slammed into the icky mud and my shoe continued to roll. Pain burned through the muscle which lived in the back of my ankle. My hip hit the ground first, and I jolted to a sudden stop, my butt firmly in the ditch.

I clutched my sore ankle, wincing at the slight pressure. Holy mother of Jesus it ached.

Pushing my palms into the wet ground, I tried to get mobile, but the pain darting through my foot was too much. At least for right now.

"You didn't have to feign an injury to get out of racing, M." Jordan jumped down into the ditch, splashing water up into my face. "What'd you do?"

"My ankle. It rolled and—ouch!" Fire-laced pain burst through that damn muscle as Jordan lifted the affected foot. "Don't touch it."

He let the limb go and it dropped into the water,

my heel slamming against the base of the trench. I screamed out in pain and Jordan fell to the side, replaced by a black-Akubra-wearing wannabe cowboy. "I've got her."

Jordan jumped over to my other side and slipped an arm around my waist. "We're okay, man. Come on, Molly. I'm gonna help you up on three. One—"

"I said I've got her." Callan levelled a hard look at my friend.

Jordan stared him down. "And who the fuck are you?"

"You can both back the hell off. I'm alright."

Jordan gave me a sceptical look and let go, but Callan's arm replaced my friend's, sliding underneath my back. He lifted me out of the ditch to a freaking audience; the Sullivan brothers both gawked from the course's side. And as for the other townsfolk, half of them were still at the water hauler, the rest scattered between here and there as if they'd raced after the man whose chest I was smooshed against. And worst of all, Callie-May stood by the fire truck with not an iota of mud to be seen on her too-pretty dress as she watched on.

"Put me down," I hissed.

"Don't think so, sweetheart. Can you even bear weight on that ankle?"

"Of course I can."

Totally ignoring me, he walked all the way to the fire truck before he set me on the ground against the huge wheel, then he squatted beside me. Deep eyes peered into mine and that freckle just under Callan's left eye shifted as he frowned. "Which one?"

"Which what?" I snapped.

Gentle fingers brushed my left foot, and my heart

felt as if it were holding its breath. Pity the flutters in my tummy wouldn't do the same thing.

Callan's hand moved to my other foot and gently unlaced the jogger. Clenching my molars, I blocked out the hurt and focused on that swirly feeling in my stomach instead. Soft fingers brushed over my bare skin and the swirls escalated, which was a damn fine thing as removing the tight sock stung like the devil. "It's a bit swollen," he said, cradling the stupid foot in his hands.

Leaning forward to better see, I winced as my foot slipped a fraction.

"I see you've still got the co-ordination of a newborn foal." Callie-May leaned over Callan's shoulder, her white-blonde hair brushing his neck. "Did you trip over those clown-sized feet?"

Callan swatted her dyed mane away. "Piss off, Callie-May."

She moved further into his space. "Oh Molly." She tutted. "I see you're still chasing after guys who are way out of your league."

Déjàvu slammed into me. *Callie-May in full-bitch mode, Callan standing up for me.*

This had happened before.

Placing my foot atop the discarded shoe, Callan leaned forward and fitted his palm around my cheek. "No, Callie-May; it's Molly who's a long way above your league."

His mouth grazed over my lips, and if it wasn't for the wheel of the truck against my back I would've fallen over for sure.

NINE

Warm lips rested against my own, not moving, not kissing, just sitting there, as if it were the most natural thing in the world. As if they belonged. As if they'd been there before.

Oh. My. Holyfreakingheartbeat.

Callan was the guy from that night. My head spun as tingles crept up my spine.

"You ... you ..." Where the hell had my voice gone? The swirls finally stopped their fluttering assault on my tummy as I slid my hands behind his neck and my fingers into his hair then tugged, forcing his face away from mine. "You're him."

His mouth crept into that arrogantly stupid semi-smile.

He knew exactly what I was talking about? How long had he known and not said anything while I practically swooned at his feet? I took a breath and forced myself to look him in the eye, ignoring the cute-as-hell freckle a thumb's span from its corner.

Distance ... I needed to process this without his presence making my head fuzzy. I pushed up off the ground. My knee hit him smack in the chest and Callan tumbled backwards, his butt hitting the dust.

Pain knifed through my foot, but I gritted my teeth and took one hobbling step then another.

"Molly."

I held my chin high and kept limping away as fast as I could, my arms tucked into my sides.

"Molly." Callan ran past me and swung around to block my path. "You've been running away since I met you. It's time to stop."

I didn't look at him as I hobbled past, just kept my chin high and my gaze set on the stables.

He clutched my elbow. "I never realised how drunk you were that night. Hell, how messed up we both were, or I wouldn't have let things go as far as they did. But when you showed up here and didn't recognise me ..." he stopped for a breath, "... it was a second chance."

His other hand cupped my jaw and Callan stepped forward until the brim of his hat shaded my eyes from the bright sun. His lips were once again almost on mine; the heat of his exhale brushed my cheek. That hand firmed around the side of my face and he tilted his lips until they hovered over my mouth. "May I?"

My tummy clenched, my heart jumped, and my mouth flooded with need. My aching foot rose off the ground just as we made contact. And the contact was delicious. Light at first, his mouth barely brushed against mine, but then it made a second, closer sweep. Rough stubble grazed my chin, but it was my lips that screamed out, and their cry was for more. More of Callan. On the third pass I smashed my mouth over his, not letting him sweep past again. Holding still wasn't enough, so I kissed him, really kissed him, by deepening our connection with my tongue. As if it were the signal he'd been waiting for, Callan's other hand landed on the small of my back and he pulled me against him. His tongue, warm and firm, slid against mine while my insides turned to absolute mush.

You be careful around him.

My mother's words kick-started my brain.

Tamping down the fuzzy feelings, I extracted myself from the sexiest guy this side of Hollywood and half-jokingly called him out for what he'd done.

"You don't just take a girl's virginity then pretend it never happened."

His eyes widened and he reached for my hand. Why in the hell did I say the *V* word?

"Took your virginity?" Callan frowned.

"Molly!" Olivia's voice cut through the thick air, and I turned away from him to face her.

"Molly," Callan squeezed my hands and I swung back around. "We fooled around that night, but I'm pretty sure we both passed out before things got too heavy. We didn't have sex. Your virginity's intact—"

"You're a virgin?" Liv bustled up beside me

I pulled away from Callan. Heat crept up my neck and didn't stop until it had burned the tips of my ears.

"Jordan said you got hurt." Liv's gaze fell to my naked foot. "Good heavens. That needs ice. Logan!" She turned over her shoulder, in search of her man. "Logan, come help us."

Callan cleared his throat behind us. "There's ice in the first-aid—"

Keeping my eyes firmly on my friend, not the guy

I'd totally forgotten I didn't sleep with, I asked, "Can you run me home?"

"Of course we can."

Logan appeared with Jordan at his side. The boys each placed an arm around me, and I tossed mine over their necks. The Hays brothers carried me back to Logan's car, my sore foot dangling in the air. It probably looked all kinds of ridiculous, but I really didn't care. I just wanted to put as much distance as possible between myself and that stupid black hat. It was completely selfish to drag my friends away from their fun, but once again ... distance felt more pressing than politeness. I'd never been more embarrassed in my life.

TEN

The Monday after the mud run the door squeaked open, and without shifting my attention from the rerun of *Neighbours*, I said, "Check out that actor from *House M.D.* How young is he there?" I couldn't remember the guy's name, but my parents had watched all eight seasons of the medical show. The young doctor he portrayed was a long shot from the love-struck high school kid he had played on the home-grown soap. "Seems like everyone started out on *Neighbours* or *Home and Away*."

The door clicked closed and frowning, I turned to look over the back of the couch, keeping my foot propped on the coffee table. My mother stood by the closed door, a grocery bag in hand and a sour look on her face.

The buzzer from downstairs sounded, and I held up a hand as I pushed myself off the couch. "Hold that thought."

"I'll get it." Mum placed her bag on the floor and

slipped back through the door she'd just closed.

Already on my foot—singular, because the other was wrapped in a tight bandage—I hopped over to the door and grabbed the green shopping bag. Peering inside was irresistible, and stealing a piece of peppermint slice was too tempting. I probably would have pinched some of the sweets if it wasn't for the sound of giggling downstairs.

Resting my bung foot against the frame, I cracked the door to check who it was. A bunch of young women filled the reception area, their short shorts and midriff tops no doubt giving my mother an ulcer. The girl at the counter leaned over it, swiping her credit card through the machine while her friends hung back, and that was where the giggling came from.

"It's not fair you got the best room. Mine was a bit ..."

I paused breathing, dying to hear what she had to say, certain the words would be whispered.

"... trashy."

My gaze flew to my mother, whose lips had pursed as if she'd heard, too. Sure our rooms were outdated, but trashy? Not a descriptor I would have considered.

"Next year, I'm booking the room you had."

Blondie laughed. "That's if there is a next year."

"The County Mud Challenge was amazing. These things always go annual when they're good."

"True that. How hard was it getting a park? I almost lost you at the end in all the hot, muddy people."

"Safe journey, girls. I hope we see you again." Mum gave the exiting guests her cheeriest smile, which didn't waver until the door had swung shut behind their backs, the overhead bell jingling their exit. She slumped onto the stool, worry creasing her brow.

I sat on the top stair and watched them climb into a new-looking hatchback. "I—"

"You told me so?" Mum sighed as she filed their paperwork into the drawer then slammed it shut. "Maybe it *is* time for an upgrade."

My gaze drifted toward the velvet drapes. "Dad and I just want this motel to do well."

"I know. Spending that sort of money isn't possible though, even if the bank hadn't knocked us back ..." Her lips thinned again, and I shuffled my weight to prop my sore foot on top of the good one. Keeping her eyes on the desk, Mum asked, "What happened on Sunday?"

I frowned. "I told you already. I landed wrong and twisted my ankle."

She shuffled a stack of papers on the reception desk. "You arrived with one boy, were seen kissing another and ..."

"What?" I pushed myself back into a standing position and hobbled down the four stairs to the front desk. Heat flared in my face as the memory of Callan's kiss slammed into my mouth.

"Tell me, Molly, did he force himself on you?"

"What? No! No one forced themselves on me." The feel of his hands on my face sent my tummy to tingling and oh my lord. My virginity was intact, but I looked like an idiot who couldn't hold her drink, let alone her memories. "Not on Sunday or ever."

Shaking her head, Mum dropped onto the tall stool behind the desk as if she were exhausted. "I just don't know how to keep you safe anymore. That boy is bad news."

"This is ridiculous." I threw my hands in the air. "Callan's just a guy, Mum, a really sweet guy. He's not some rapist."

Her face paled.

"And nor is Jordan. Shit, he's sixteen, for goodness sake. He's probably still a virgin." Or not ... She didn't need to know about the string of girls Liv said the young footy player brought home. "Why are you so freaking prudish? It's not like I sleep around." *Ha!* "I have guys who are friends—that does not make me a harlot, and even if I was ..."

Shaking my head, I pushed past her and ran outside. My foot didn't feel too bad with a little weight, but as I extracted the basher's key from my pocket and climbed in the old car, I realised working the clutch might be a problem. *Ah, screw it.* I started the engine and jammed my heel down on the clutch. The pain wasn't too bad. It was almost bearable, so I reversed out of the parking space and shoved the car into first then careened up the driveway, pulling it to a sharp stop at the turn onto the main road.

You're running away.

Damn it. Maybe I was. Maybe I wanted to. Maybe ...

May-goddamn-be!

I yanked the gearstick into reverse, and the tyres squealed as I backed into the parking lot. The basher rumbled its complaint and I dropped my forehead onto the steering wheel. My anger had been looking to escape since the amazing kiss Callan and I had shared on Saturday morning. Using numb fingers, I turned the key in the ignition, killing the engine. I wouldn't run away from my mother. From her accusations. But from Callan ...? My arms curled around my tummy. I felt naked at the fact he'd known all this time and I hadn't even realised I hadn't had sex that night, let alone that he was the mystery guy.

I took a deep breath in through my nose and blew out a long exhale, then I opened the door and climbed out. My mother still stood behind the front counter, and when I entered her shoulders squared up and a flat expression crossed her face. "I just want what's best for you."

"I'm a grown woman, Mum. You have to let me figure some things out by myself."

Her lips puckered as if that were hard to swallow. I kept my distance, leaning against the window to relieve my foot of a little weight. She didn't look at me, just focused on whatever she was doing on the computer, as if I was of no consequence. Apparently I was safe enough now there were no men around. I sighed, bit my bottom lip, and twirled my fingers around one another.

"One of my uni friends is about to graduate with a Bachelor of Business Studies. He even runs his own shop. Maybe I can give him a call to talk about this place. He could have some ideas about how we can spruce things up on the cheap."

Mum glanced away from her work for barely a second. "I'm not taking advice from some young upstart student who knows nothing about running a motel."

The bell jingled, and I threw my hands into the air again.

Dad moseyed through the front door, took in my frazzled state and pulled me into a one-armed hug. "I'm going downtown for some lunch. Do you want to come?"

I glanced at my frustrating mother. "Hell yes."

"Want anything, Patty?"

Mum glanced up, offering her husband a small smile. "No thanks."

I slipped out the door and waited just outside for what felt like forever. Dad finally appeared and slapped my shoulder. "We might drive today, Mols."

"Sure." I gave him the best smile I could muster. We never drove. It was a glorious waste of fuel, or so Mum said, when walking to just about anywhere in town took no longer than fifteen minutes. Dad offered his arm, and I gratefully placed a little weight on it as we made our way to the family wagon, which hid in the back corner of the Akuna's parking lot. An older model, the paintwork was peeling off just like the motel's walkways. I guess money had been tight for longer than I'd realised.

We opened all the doors and stood there for a few moments, waiting for the heat to rush out. Even though I expected him to ask what had gone down with Mum, he never did.

"We got another compliment on room ten this morning."

"Yeah?" He leaned inside and started the engine.

"Aha. Those girls that stayed the extra day after the mud run had two rooms. The ones in nine weren't happy their friends scored the good suite."

He grinned at me. "That's great news."

I grinned back.

The engine rumbled its complaint at idling as the fan worked overtime to clear the hot air. Dad tapped the roof. "With all those extra guests over the weekend, we would have made a few dollars. Let's look at some more paint to start fixing up the other rooms."

Ducking, Dad sat in the driver's seat, and I lowered myself into the other side. In a few minutes' time we pulled up out front of the hardware store, and it might have been premature to spend money that hadn't yet hit the bank, but excitement thrummed through me.

We both climbed out and walked through the front door.

"Hi Molly. Mr McLean." Callie-May's irritating voice ruined the good vibe I finally had going. "What can I help you both with today?" She smiled far more sweetly than she really was.

"We're just browsing, thanks Callie. Maybe picking up some paint." Dad walked toward the back wall, which held cans of paint.

"Wasn't the mud run fabulous on the weekend?"

Great. She'd followed us.

"Delightful," I answered.

"Callan Hunter is doing wonderful things out there at Bellevue. I suppose you know all about the planned retreat, working there and all. Horse riding and accommodation ... it's going to be a massive change when it's all done. Why, the mud run was just the beginning, huh? Soon not much of the old farm will remain."

Change? Retreat?

Where in the hell were they putting enough accommodation for a retreat and why, oh why, did this town need even more empty rooms to fill? I'd been at Bellevue for weeks now and no one had said anything about those kinds of changes. My stomach churned with the news, but it was okay. It had to be.

I'd still have the creek.

ELEVEN

No matter how badly I didn't want to see Callan, I couldn't stay away from Bellevue forever. I needed the money work provided and didn't want to lose time with Jed. When at college, I missed the old horse something fierce, so needed to suck up all his affection now. Or maybe I did want to see Callan, because my heart tickled my ribs every time I so much as thought his name, but that only lasted until I realised what was happening. Then embarrassment pushed everything else aside.

It had been three days since I'd hurt my ankle at the mud run and it was feeling much better, so I couldn't use the injury as an excuse to avoid the stables any longer. I pulled the basher into its spot under the huge gum and climbed out. I'd actively not taken notice of who was walking around the east paddock as I drove up the long drive, just like I hadn't seen that construction guy's truck leaving, and I hadn't watched a certain Akubra tip in greeting as

I'd passed. Nor had I noticed him in my rear-vision mirror.

Entering the stable, I resolved to ignore that dark-haired someone and everything he stood for. Maybe Mum was right.

Or completely wrong.

But that didn't bear thinking about.

In his stable, Jed stood at the feed bucket, munching on a new biscuit of hay. I let myself in and noticed that fresh water filled his trough. His coat shone like he'd recently been groomed, and the straw in his stall didn't smell. Not a single pile of manure was anywhere to be seen. I gave the big guy a few slaps on the neck, just as he liked, then ruffled the soft hair between his ears. Trail rides were a good thing. Bellevue would still need horses, and therefore still need stables. Hopefully that meant they wouldn't make too many changes to my pop's building, and that Jed could stay on. It wasn't my business or my choice after all.

I dropped my forehead onto Jed's neck. The familiar smell of horse and hay was almost enough to undo me, but I was too strong for that today.

Still leaning against the huge grey I pulled out my phone and fired off a text to Liv.

Miss you

"How's the foot?"

I near jumped out of my skin at Callan's voice in my space. Turning around, I slipped my phone into the pocket of my jean shorts and pressed my back against Jed's side.

"Better."

Callan's gaze lingered on the gummy foot, riskily clad in a sandal, before all-too-slowly sliding up to meet my eyes. My damn chest held a freaking dance party, and crap, this guy had such a strong effect on me. Maybe it was the raging hormones I couldn't seem to get in check since *that* night, or maybe it was something else, but whatever it was, I needed to get a grip.

"Why are you avoiding me?" He took a step closer, and I squared my shoulders, meeting him eye to eye.

My phone vibrated against my butt, its ring filling the stuffy stable. I let it buzz away. Callan arched a brow. "You going to get that?"

Holding his stare, I reached into my back pocket and flipped open the cover then picked up without checking the screen. "What is it?"

"Nice way to great someone you miss dearly."

I sighed. "Liv."

"Everything okay?"

"Yeah ... I just ..." I looked at my dirty toes sticking out the end of my sandal.

"You sound flustered."

"It's nothing." I sighed again, bringing my eyes back to Callan, who still held me in his gaze. "Just facing down an impossible ..."

Callan grinned and lifted his dumb hat, as if he was proud of the fact he had me all worked up, again. My molars ground together.

"Put him on the phone."

"What the hell, Liv?"

"I want to talk to this guy Jordan said got all territorial—"

"No way." I could see exactly where this was

going, and I wasn't having a bar of it.

"Molly ..."

"Olivia."

"Please?" Argh. She wasn't Savvy; Liv was as nice as they came. Surely she wouldn't make this more embarrassing than it already was.

"Fine," I said, holding the phone out to Callan. "She wants to talk to you."

"Really?" That stupid conceited smile curled his mouth. A mouth with lips so soft and skilled—I jammed the phone into his hand.

"Hi there." He kept smiling. "Aha." Nodding. "Absolutely." His gaze dropped to my lips, and my tummy heated. I toed the straw with my Doc-covered foot, pushing it into a hollow circle, and when I looked up his eyes continued wandering over me. "She's a great girl. Full of fire, but a bit of spark isn't going to scare me off." He winked at me, then chuckled. "Yeah. Will do."

Maybe God was smiting me now for that night at the B&S.

"Nice talking to you ..." His brows dipped for a moment before rising as a huge smile split his face. "Olivia."

He held the phone out and I snatched it up real fast, bringing it to my ear. "What was that?"

"Nothing," Liv said. "Now, New Year's—I have to work, but the boys said they'd come out and collect you. We're not doing anything huge, just a barbeque and party here. Savvy and Dane are coming across, and I think Cade might be in town ... or maybe not. Don't bring anything, okay? I've got it all covered."

Jed's skin shivered beneath my back and my hand dropped to my side, idly scratching his thigh. "It's too far for Logan to come all the way out here and get me. It's nearly two hours."

"It's *only* two hours, Molly, and he doesn't mind. It'll give him and Jordan a chance to chat."

"I can't come, even though I'd really love to see everyone."

Liv shut me down. "Hush. You're coming."

"I could take you." My attention flew to the hot-as-hell cowboy standing less than three feet away. "Wherever it is you want to go, I'll take you."

I shook my head at him as I spoke into the phone. "I've got to go. We'll talk soon."

"Love you, girl."

"You too, Liv."

I ended the call and pushed the phone back into my pocket, directing my next words to Callan. "Thank you, but no."

Ducking around his bulk, I slipped through the stable gate and made for the tack room. Whoever had looked after my horse had seen to all the others as well, so I tossed my bag in the corner of the musty concrete room and grabbed Jed's bridle off its peg, then hefted his saddle onto my arm, along with a saddle blanket. As I stepped out into the dusty stable, Callan looked up from where he was still standing in the entry to my horse's pen.

"Excuse me." I shuffled past him and placed the saddle over the railing of the gate. Callan watched me get the horse ready for a ride. Honestly, it was a bit unnerving the way he just stood there, staring, not saying a word. Surely the man had work to do, or something. Anything other than loitering here, which magnified my embarrassment.

Bustling past him again, I hit the tack room and

closed its door behind me. I unlaced my Doc and slipped it off. Unzipping my tight shorts, I let them fall to the floor and stepped out, then fished around the bottom of my backpack for my jeans. A ride was in order to get away from it all. Just letting Jed take the reins would be so relaxing. Besides, my horse would need the release after being penned up for a few days.

The wood panelled door swung open.

I looked that way and shot straight up, jeans in hand. Callan stood frozen, his hand on the wide open door. His dark eyes dropped from my face and I just freaking stood there, unable to move, my bare legs on display. Hell, my black and pink polka dot knickers on display.

"Get out!" I crossed the three strides to the door and shoved him away, then slammed the stupid thing closed. Tugging my jeans on so fast my good foot caught in the ends, I yanked and twisted and fell to the ground. "Damn it."

The door flew open again.

"You okay?"

"Get out!" This time, Callan smiled before closing the door himself.

I was so flustered it took three goes to get the zipper up and the button closed, but finally I had my pants on and my shoes back in place. My face still felt like a furnace when I opened the tack room door, and oh crap, Callan hadn't moved from the other side.

"I—ah—" I shook my head. There was no point in even trying to talk to him right now. Not when he'd just seen me half-naked.

"Molly ..." His hand closed around my own and drawing a slow breath, I shut my eyes, thinking of whatever the hell I could to ease the embarrassment of whatever witty comment was coming my way.

"What are you actually doing here?" I opened my eyes, and his gaze slipped off mine. "Well?"

After at least a minute with still no answer, I sucked my cheek into the space between my top and bottom teeth and walked away. Tossing his head around, Jed was more than ready to hit the road, so I opened up his stall and kicked my good foot into the high stirrup, then hoisted myself onto the horse's back. My big grey walked through the door without prompting, and once out of the stables he pulled at the bit and picked up the pace. I guess he'd missed our rides the past few days.

"I'm trying to make a difference."

I peeped over my shoulder, and Angel trotted along behind us with Callan swamping her thirteen-hand frame. The bay pony trotted to catch up to Jed's long strides, and I held serious fears for Callan's man parts as he bounced on her bare back. I nudged Jed into a trot and Angel broke into a canter. The smoother gait would have to be easier on Callan's butt. Only he didn't exactly look at home on the little pony. Flapping his elbows like a berserk chicken, it looked as if he were in peril of slipping right off her back and he hadn't even replaced his black hat with a safety helmet.

"Grip with your knees," I warned. "And your feet. You need to use everything you've got to hold on."

Yeah, that wasn't helping. Without warning Angel slowed her pace and settled back into a speedy trot. Callan slipped to the side and his arms shot out, circling around her neck. His chest pressed against her wither, and I would have laughed if it weren't for his knees slipping ... slipping ... slipping down one of her sides and up the other.

And he was gone.

Tugging on the reins, I pulled Jed to a halt and threw my leg over his side, sliding to the ground.

Callan pushed himself up off the grass and retrieved his hat from where it had fallen. He dusted the felt off and popped it back on his head. "Good thing I didn't have too far to fall."

Suppressing a smile, I said, "I thought you knew horses."

He broke eye contact to look at Angel who'd wound up a few metres away, and now stood munching on the long grass. "I know horses."

"But you can't ride."

"Not exactly."

I offered my hand and Callan took it, so I pulled him to his feet. Without releasing his hold, he said, "I've ridden a few times before."

"But never without a saddle, right?" A laugh bubbled to the surface and spluttering, I let it out. He grinned right back at me. Not that stupidly arrogant smirk he was so fond of, but a real, almost-embarrassed smile. Maybe I wasn't the only one looking strange. Embarrassment could creep up on anyone and that smile made him look somehow sexier than he ever had.

"Honestly, I'm more at home on a subway."

"'Cause those two things are exactly alike."

"Okay then, a scooter."

I laughed again, my hand still in his. "Go home, city boy."

He tipped his hat and smirked. "Country kid, through and through."

Yeah, I could see right through that lie. "And I'm a classy city girl."

He squeezed my hand. *Shit, my hand.* I let it fall from his and rushed forward to snag Angel's reins. In a few slow strides Callan relieved me of her, and I didn't bother climbing back up onto Jed, but rather led him as I walked. Callan and Angel fell into step beside us.

"You love this place, huh?"

I didn't know how to answer that, so I didn't, but the silence that stretched between us wasn't awkward. It felt so comfortable, the likes of which I hadn't felt with another person in this place since I came here with my grandfather.

"My pop used to bring me fishing down here when I was little. It was his favourite spot. One time ..." I glanced across at Callan as we walked, "we caught an eel catfish. It was almost half a metre long, and I hooked it on the little hand reel he'd rigged up. I didn't have what it took to haul the thing in, so he jumped in the creek and caught it in his hands then tossed it up onto the bank beside me." I smiled at the memory. "We told Grandma I caught that one."

Callan shifted his hat forward so it shaded his face. "I'm really not trying to take anything away from what's already at Bellevue."

"Then what *are* you doing?"

"We're talking about making it a family-friendly retreat. Trail rides through the mountains, campfires around the creek. Maybe some chalets."

Chalets were a pretty big venture ... "What about the ponies that agist?"

He passed me a serious look. "Jed will always have a place here."

Somehow we found ourselves down by the creek in the back paddock, with Angel and Jed grazing on the semi-green grass by the water.

Callan shifted his feet, crossing one ankle over the other. "You should have told me."

I snapped off a long piece of paspalum and curled it around my finger. "Told you what?"

"That you were a virgin. I didn't know."

Oh, my ... My tummy swished, churned, and my next breath rushed in. "What, kissed you, then pulled away to say, excuse me absolute stranger, but if you're thinking of screwing me tonight you probably should know I'm a virgin." I laughed. "Who actually says stuff like that?"

"It was so hard to do the right thing and put a stop to it that night. Your body ..." He swallowed. "But now, I'm so damn glad I did. Your first time should be special."

"Was yours?"

He frowned at me.

"I'm so tired of these double standards, Callan. Why can't a girl be in charge of her own sexuality and how she wants to lose *it,* just like guys are? Who are you to say I didn't want to break my hymen in the back of a truck, half plastered, with some guy I'd never met before?"

Callan picked up a stone and tossed it into the creek. "I'm glad we didn't do it that night."

There wasn't a lot more to say. We fell into silence, and Callan's quiet company made me forget about the Akuna's problems, and miss my friends less. There was something almost settling about sitting by the creek with him by my side. He never made a move above letting our shoulders rest against one another, and by the time we returned to the stables an hour later, I felt as if maybe I had a new friend.

TWELVE

Christmas came, went, and was a non-event. The motel remained empty, my friends all rang to pass on their greetings, and I visited the stables like it was any other day. All week, Bellevue remained oddly quiet in a way it never had before. It wasn't that there hadn't been times in the past when I was the only one about, but usually, I didn't notice or care. This year though, it felt like I was the lone occupant floating around a ghost town. I guess holidays were like that. Everyone got busy. That was probably why I didn't see hide nor hat of Callan, even now almost a week later. Sometime around Christmas Eve he'd vanished without warning, and even though we were probably only friends, I had kind of wanted to swap numbers. Being around him mightn't be a blush-fest anymore, but I was still curious as to why he hadn't mentioned the B&S back when Joy first introduced us.

The lack of work at both the motel and stables meant I could spend entire afternoons riding across the creek and up into the base of the mountains—my special space, that in just four more years would legally be mine, thanks to the trust clause in Pop's will. Maybe I'd build myself a little house out here one day.

During that week, Jed was my constant companion. There was something about his company that made it less like being alone. Not that I'd ever had a problem with being alone before, but lately it seemed more noticeable. The days were warm, so I finished up with my feet in the creek more often than not.

Studying the pebbles visible through the crystal-clear water, I wriggled my bare toes in its cool embrace. Finding the perfect skipping stone sometimes took forever. I nudged a flat one with my toes, tipping it over, but the bottom wasn't anywhere near smooth enough. It'd only taken a single afternoon when I was six for Pop to teach me how to skim stones across the top of the creek. "A perfectly flat rock," he'd said, "no bigger than the palm of my hand, when thrown just right will skip as if it's jumping along the water's surface." I smiled, remembering the countless rocks that had sunk straight to the bottom when I'd hoicked them. Pop had even thrown a few duds too.

"You beauty."

What in the *what*? I swung around, looking for the voice that I'd missed almost as much as my buddies. Buddies I'd be seeing in just one more day.

"Sounds like a sure thing."

It was coming from ... the other side of the creek? I pushed off my rock seat, and peered into the scrub on the other bank while cool water lapped at my ankles.

"Yeah ... yeah, it won't be a problem."

The black hat he loved to wear covered his face from sight as he glanced at the water, holding a phone to his ear.

My gaze traced over the rocks a little way downstream. It wasn't a wide creek. I could probably jump across it by landing on a few of the bigger river rocks that jutted out of the surface.

"Hey you."

My attention jumped from the rocks I'd been considering to the guy across the creek. One of those gorgeous smiles lit up his face and I returned the motion, coupled with a wave. "Where have you been?"

"Ah." He tapped the side of his nose as he shouted across the water. "You missed me."

"No." I searched the clear water around my feet for a nice skimming rock, ignoring the pang of disappointment that he'd disappeared without even asking for my number.

"But I missed you." A thud, followed by a second, then a third filled the peaceful air. I plucked up a flat stone, smooth as Callan's talking. I'd heard the way Dane spoke to Savvy and even though I craved that type of connection, never in a million years would I have thought the sweet talk was normal. Callan was beginning to make me second guess my opinion though. He always spoke sweet and never seemed to follow it up with wanting anything from me. That didn't mean I didn't want to give him something, and right now the undeniable urge to throw myself against him made me want to give him a little more than just *something*.

He landed on my side of the creek and dropped onto the bank, where his fingers moved to slip off his cowboy boots.

Aha. I plucked up a second, perfect stone. "You barely know me; cut the flattery."

Callan hissed in air between his teeth. "Burn."

The water lapped at my rolled up jeans as I waded through the creek and back to the shore, where I plonked myself on a little cliff that dropped off into the clear water. Turning the rock over in my hands, I wondered about that night at the B&S ball. *Again.* "Why'd you pretend you didn't remember?"

Callan cleared his throat and the dry grass rustled with his shuffle.

"Because ..."

"That's not an answer."

Holding the larger of the two stones flat, I skipped it along the water, watching it hop once, twice, three times before sinking below the surface.

"Jack and Coke." His smooth voice caressed the words as if they were dangerous.

"Jack and Coke." The guy beside me ordered a drink.

I threw back another shot of Sambuca and slammed the empty glass down on the makeshift bar, giving my head a quick shake to dispel the fiery burn. The marquee wall swam in my vision for a moment, the buzz of voices fading out then back in.

I hadn't spoken to a soul all night. Despite the huge tent being filled with hundreds of people, there didn't seem to be anyone around. I must have been the only loser who'd come to this thing alone.

A quick adjustment of the strap on my borrowed dress and that was it. I'd go out on the dance floor, and I'd have a great time.

"Lone Wolf McLean ..."

My tummy clenched at the voice spawned right out of hell, and I raised my gaze from my cute flats to the shrewd eyes of my high school tormentor. Dressed in a shiny red number that glittered with each breath, Callie-May looked as stunning as ever. Fake too. Her white-blonde hair was twisted up into some kind of fancy bun, and so much makeup coated her face she'd probably used a bricklayer's trowel to slather it on.

"Callie-May." I tried to smile.

Her gaze slipped to my borrowed shoes, then examined every inch of me all the way to my braided hair, lingering on my grandma's cameo necklace. "I see nothing's changed with you. Still a loser."

"And I see you're still a cow."

"Still a friendless loner."

"Get stuffed, Callie-May. You know nothing about me."

"I know your chances of picking up an eligible bachelor tonight are ... umm ... let me see ... non-existent."

"The eligible bachelors can bite my arse and so can you, because that's not what these balls are about."

She glanced toward her friend and they both laughed. "I thought nerds were supposed to be smart. What do you think B&S stands for?"

"Bull and shit."

A heavy arm fell around my shoulders. The spicy masculine cologne tickled my senses as a gravelly voice said, "There you are, baby."

Stubble grazed my chin as a pair of tender lips landed on my own. Strong fingers glided up my spine and tangled in the hair at the back of my neck. He smiled against my mouth, and his tongue skated over the seam of my lips.

The stranger broke our kiss, turning side on and tugging me into the space against his hip as he shifted his attention to Callie-May. "Sorry ... ahh ..."

Frowning, she snapped her gaping mouth closed. "You know exactly who I am."

She spun on her heel and clomped off, the fast clip of her high heels making the exit look haughty.

A deep chuckle shook the body I was leaning against, and I extracted myself from his hold, watching as my former tyrant stalked away. Twisting around to get a good look at the guy, I noticed it was the same one who'd been at the bar drinking Jack and Coke.

His mouth curled in that way only a certain type of person could pull off. It made anyone else look like a smirking super villain. "You're welcome."

"Excuse me?"

"For the kiss."

"I didn't need your help to get rid of Callie-May."

I turned away and made for the dance floor. Squeezing into a free space, I shimmied along to the music. Fire lit up my veins, sending a crazy buzz through my head, and good lord, I could do anything. Be anyone. No one here knew what I was really like. Who I really was deep inside. It'd been three years since high school, and well, a lot could change in that time. I wasn't the socially inept school dux anymore, nor was I an easy target.

I'd only been dancing for a few minutes before I felt that uncomfortable sensation of someone watching me. Trying to play it cool, I continued moving, holding my hands in the air while I danced. Callie-May could get stuffed. I wasn't going to let her get to me.

The feeling didn't fade, but that wasn't going to dampen my fun. After a few songs, my throat felt dry, so I headed toward my earlier perch and that's when I saw him again.

Mr Jack and Coke pushed off the bar, leaving the dude he'd been talking with. His gaze focused on me. Me? A small smile tipped the very corners of his mouth and goodness, this guy oozed confidence. He stepped right into my personal space, so close the heat of his body coated mine.

"You can't just kiss strangers like that." I tipped my head back to meet his gaze. "Kiss me like that."

"Says who?" His lips parted. "You?"

My head buzzed. My heart thumped as if it were mid-marathon. Even my legs felt kind of weak. He cocked an eyebrow, and his hand slipped up my arm, over my shoulder. Fingers brushed against the thin strap of my dress and trailed over the sensitive skin of my neck, and I shuddered.

With his hand cupping my jaw, he asked again, "You?"

My tongue, huge and wet, refused to work. My tingling lips couldn't speak. He dipped his head, his lips dusted mine, and I shuddered again. The short pause would have been opportunity to deny him, but I didn't. His mouth passed over mine once more then again, the fourth time resting in place. I relaxed a little, drawing the breath I hadn't realised I was detaining.

"No." My admission came on an unsteady exhale.

Then he kissed me so thoroughly my fingers curled into his shirt. When he broke away, it felt like I was drowning. I drew in an unsteady breath and in a move more gutsy than I would normally dare, I slipped my fingers between his and dragged that handsome stranger onto the dance floor. And oh-em-gee, did he know how to work it. Although I loved dancing, I'd always felt like an uncoordinated elephant when I danced with someone else, but the way this guy included me in his moves made me feel as if we owned the floor. Everyone watched us for the right reasons, not because I was stepping on his toes. Sliding a hand onto his back, I pulled him against me, and our bodies moved together for song after song after song.

Eventually, we made it back to the bar, where this time, we both did a shot of Sambuca. Leaning back against the portable counter, I threw back my second glass of the fiery liquid. My stranger stepped forward, angling his body against mine and wow, the feeling that slammed into my stomach was undeniable. His lips hovered above the glistening skin on my neck and I shivered.

Everything blurred into sensation. Hot pulses, cold shivers, tingling skin under warm fingers. Then the memories fizzled out ...

...

...

...

Until hot lips danced on mine. My hips ground against his to the beat of the music. Fire flowed through my veins and my head felt as if it had lost control. Need had taken over and I needed this, needed him, needed to feel. There was something about this guy that was utterly desirable. There was no other way to describe it.

Perhaps it was my Sambuca buzz. Shit, am I drunk? *I couldn't—*

Firm hands cupped my thighs and my feet automatically linked behind a solid back, resting on the curve of his firm butt. I shouldn't—

"I'm not. I can't—"

Hooking up with a total stranger was so sleazy.

He pulled away enough to look me in the eye for a few heartbeats. His grip on me loosened and everything inside me screamed, 'No. Don't let this end.' I slammed my needy lips back against his and clenched my legs around his middle.

Kissing me back with just as much force, he backed us away from the main marquee and my blood roared its approval.

Everything fell away again as the only thing I could see, hear, smell, touch was this guy.

Our bodies responded to each other so fiercely, and somehow we made it to the back of a truck I hoped was his, 'cause it sure as hell wasn't mine ...

"It's so soft," I murmured, gliding my hands over his shaved

head. "Not spiky at all."

"Mmm." He kissed the corner of my mouth then placed another tender kiss on its centre.

After that, nothing sweet or innocent stained the way he kissed me or the way I kissed him back. All thoughts of soft hair fell away as we lost ourselves in each other.

"Jack and Coke's not an answer."

"Because you intrigued me so much that night that I hadn't stopped thinking about you in three months. And when I saw you here, it was like fate handed me a chance to get to know you without the beer buzz. You'd bolted the morning after the ball, and be damned if I was going to give you the chance to run again."

Screw it.

I turned around to face him, and Callan continued watching me as if I were the most fascinating creature in the world. I took the two steps to close the distance between where he sat on the shore and where I stood facing him. Callan pushed himself onto his feet, and challenging my stare with a raised eyebrow, removed his hat.

It must have been the slowest, most agonising moment known to mankind, us standing there staring, asking, waiting. Finally, the tummy flutters were too much, so I grabbed him by the shoulders and pulled us together, my lips going straight to his as if we were the opposite sides of a magnetic force. I kissed him like I'd always imagined kissing should be—full of passion and need and so much emotion that he must have been able to feel the fact I'd been holding back since that night.

His hand slid up into my ponytail, his long fingers

cradling my head as he kissed me back with everything I gave him and then more. It was one of those moments where everything around us faded into nothing and even time itself became obsolete, while the only thing grounding me to that particular instant in time was the intensity of the feelings pulling the two of us together.

My hand slid under his shirt, seeking out the fire from my memories. Callan's abs tightened and his inhale hissed through the tiny space between our lips.

He pulled away. "Molly ..."

The absence of his lips made mine ache. I kissed his cheek, and moved down to the line of his jaw, trailing soft kisses all the way to his ear.

"Molly ..."

"Callan?" I pressed my lips to the throbbing pulse on his neck.

His throat tensed as he swallowed and his fingers curled around my shoulders. "Not here. Not like this."

"Yes here. Yes now. Yes you."

With my palms flat against his warm skin I kissed him as if there were no tomorrow, and he held me like our tomorrow would last forever. Our clothes wound up in a pile just as tangled as ourselves while the warm sun cast shadows over us.

THIRTEEN

It must have been near six p.m. when I pulled on my Docs. Callan's fingers trailed down my spine as I tugged the laces tight.

"You're so beautiful."

Heat rose into my cheeks, and I kept my eyes on my shoes. "We'd better get these horses to bed."

"I mean it. You are."

Happy warmth filled me from top to bottom, not missing a single space within me. Callan had been sweet and gentle, and my body was still humming with the memory of his touch. It had been everything a first time should be.

I took a deep breath and smoothed my hair back into its earlier ponytail, refastening the tie around it. "It'll be dinner time soon. I'm sure Joy will be looking for you."

Warm lips skated over the back of my neck. "Take the compliment, Molly."

Heat flushed my face again and I stood, moving to

unwrap Jed's reins from the tree branch. My tummy jittered as I focused on the leather straps.

"Why's it so hard?"

"Compliments bred awkwardness." I began picking a path away from the rocky bank so I could swing myself onto my horse's back. Callan caught my hand in his and threaded his fingers between mine. "You should never feel awkward when people speak the truth. If I tell you something honest, will you run away?"

"I don't run away."

An uneven cough made it sound like he choked on a chuckle. Our shoulders bumped together and continued to do so with every other step.

"You were bloody beautiful at the ball, but that night's got nothing on how gorgeous you are right now."

Oh my, sweet somethings. Riding back was overrated.

I squeezed my fingers around his and Callan raised my hand to his lips, pressing a kiss against my knuckles. This was a perfect first time.

"You're such a sweet talker."

"It's the honest to God truth, baby."

My heart smiled. Or at least, felt like a smile should—all warm and soft. The sinking sun made our shadows stretch across the long grass, and seeing the two of us together in silhouette was surreal. The guy by my side couldn't possibly be the same one from the fuzzy memories I'd been fighting with for months. That was just too much like a fairytale. As we crested the hill behind the stables, I loosened my grip, but Callan's fingers tightened around my hand. "What's the hurry?"

"Dinner?" I hedged.

He chuckled as we came around the side of the stables, walking in the distended shade cast by the huge gum. Another car sat alongside the basher, its dusty paint contrasting in faded red against the dry grass. I stilled for a second. Today was definitely only December the thirtieth.

"Surprise!" Jordan jumped out of the vehicle, his hands spread in the air. "Couldn't wait any longer to see your face."

Callan's hand tightened around mine.

"Hey, Molly." Logan's gaze dropped to our entwined fingers for barely a second before returning to meet my look. "They switched Jordan's roster, so we're here a day before schedule. I thought maybe we could get an early start tomorrow and be home before his shift. That's if you can put us up for the night? I swung by your place to see you, but your mum—"

"Was rude as shit." Jordan flicked dark curls out of his face.

"Jordan!" Logan scolded.

I looked from Liv's blonde hottie to his dark-haired brother, words failing to form on my tongue.

"Come here, girl." Jordan held his arms wide again.

Dropping Callan's hand, I finally unfroze. "Guys, this is Callan Hunter."

Jordan leapt forward, his hug closing around me, and I circled my arms around his shoulders. Gee, had the kid grown? When he released his death grip and stepped back, Callan's gaze was still on me. His shoulders had risen and his broad chest puffed out as he watched Jordan.

Logan shot out a hand toward the cowboy

lookalike, and Jordan mumbled, "She was mine first."

I elbowed the little troublemaker in his ribs. "Friend."

"Whatcha doin' for New Year's?" Clasping hands with Callan, Logan directed his question that way. "You should come back with us. Meet the rest of the gang."

"That could be fun." Grinning, Callan passed me a wink.

****

The next morning, shouldering my heavy backpack, I walked down the stairs and into the front office, ready to meet the Hays boys. Hunched over a desk full of papers that looked suspiciously like overdue bills, my mother's head rested in her cupped hands. I paused mid-descent, watching her fingers push through her greying hair. She glanced up at my approach, her puffy eyes taking in my tattered jean shorts/Doc Marten combo, before skating to the front door where Logan leaned against his car exactly like he had the last time he was here. Only now, Callan was there too, his back pressed against the white cab of a huge truck.

Heaving in a laboured breath, I prepared for the boys-are-bad onslaught. But Mum plucked a bunch of tissues from the box on the counter and wiped at her nose without a word. Perhaps the fact I was leaving with a bunch of guys wasn't the cause of her current state after all.

"Everything okay?" I asked.

"It will be." Her eyes shone with tears as she offered up a pathetic excuse for a smile.

"Well ... ah ..." Two more steps and I reached the bottom, moved toward her and held out my hand to give my mum a hug. It sure looked like she could use one. She glanced at the hand I'd extended toward her. The cool expression I was so used to seeing firmed up her face, and I pulled back.

Rocking on my heels, I said, "I'll see you in a few days."

She nodded, her watery gaze flicking to the window. "Is that Joy's nephew? I warned—"

"Yep." I pushed through the front door, sending the brass bell into a dinging tizzy that drowned out her warnings.

Sporting his usual hat, and jeans nicer than he wore when working on the farm, Callan had perfected the country look I often saw in store windows. He tipped the front of his hat and offered up a semi-smile that sent my tummy into a frenzy.

"Morning, guys."

"That all you got?" Logan nodded toward my backpack.

"I'm only coming for two nights."

His mouth slipped into a smile. "That you are."

Jordan chuckled and I set my bag on the ground. "Better teach Liv how to pack while you're at our place. That girl is out of control."

I couldn't stop my gaze sliding back to Callan, even though I wasn't quite sure how to greet him after what went down between us yesterday.

"I'm coming too," Callan drawled.

"Coming?"

He tapped the side of his truck. "If you want me to?

Frowning, I glanced back to the brothers who'd

driven two hours to collect me. Logan's grin spread across his entire face and, I left like a puppy being led to the park.

Callan tilted his chin toward the pickup. "Shall we hit the road?"

"But ... but Logan just drove all this way to get me."

"You're not going to make that man ride alone are you, Molly?" Jordan said.

Two whole hours with just the two of us after we spent yesterday afternoon wrapped around each other. Heat flushed my cheeks.

"I want to talk to you."

Jordan chuckled. "Whatever you wanna call it, man."

I shot him a shut-up look and returned my gaze to Callan. "I want to talk to you, too."

"Maybe I want to hang out, too."

I smiled so big my cheeks ached. Logan caught my attention with a nod toward the back of his car. As he walked around, he held me in his gaze. "Do you have a problem with this bloke tagging along?"

I pressed my lips together, but the smile wouldn't tone down. "No, no, of course not."

"I'm sorry. I should have checked with you before dishing out invites." Sliding a key into the boot, he popped the back open and laid my backpack inside. "You don't have to ride with him. Just say the word."

Crazy as Logan going back empty-handed was, I really wanted to ride with Callan. My fluttering tummy agreed.

"It's cool."

He gave a single nod and pulled down the boot, then patted my arm before moving around to the driver's side. "See you there." Logan grinned then disappeared into his car, followed by a smirking Jordan who piped up with, "No parking along the way."

"Jordan!"

My shout made him laugh. As they backed out of the parking lot, I walked around to the passenger side and climbed up into Callan's monster-sized car, and my tummy fluttered. Just what did he want to say about yesterday? About the unabashed sex we'd had by the creek ...

Coming out of the driveway, we pulled onto Mount Ingalls Road and headed out of town. By the time we reached the open road, Callan had settled into a relaxed pose, one hand on the wheel, his other resting on the window.

"So yesterday ..."

Good Lord, kill me now. Nervous energy zinged through my fingers and my gaze dropped to where they twisted the frayed denim at the edge of my shorts.

A deep chuckle came from the other side of the car. "Hells, you're adorable. C'mere."

He moved his free hand to the wheel and set the other one on my knee, palm up. I glanced at him, and Callan wriggled his fingers, so I placed my palm in his. The warmth of his rough skin was sweet against my sweaty palms. "There's your pretty smile."

Sheesh, sweaty palms. The urge to pull away and swipe them clean had my fingers twitching, but I couldn't drop his hand. I didn't want to not being feeling him. But wait, I was smiling? I *was* smiling ... The warmth inside me couldn't be denied. "Joy and Marshall were okay with you running off to

Armidale?"

He winked and squeezed my hand. "You bet."

A few kilometres out of town, we passed a huge field of tall lucerne with Mount Ingalls looming in the background. "Weird-looking peak." Callan tilted his head toward the biggest mountain in the national park. Completely flat, a huge rock marked the top.

"Yeah, Dad and I have hiked it a few times. Eagle Rock's pretty amazing up close."

We settled into silence and my mind wandered away from the feel of our physical connection and back to Mum's upset state. It had to have been the bills ... things must be getting worse. But with the extra business generated from the mud run surely things were at least a little better than they had been.

The ring of Callan's phone buzzed through the car's speakers, and he extracted his hand from mine to hit the Bluetooth button on the steering wheel.

"Hello."

"They're going to sell." Marshall's voice buzzed with excitement, and Callan slapped the wheel.

"Perfect."

"When you get back, it'll be busy times."

"Of course." He tapped his fingers off the wheel as if ticking off a list. "Get Ryland Johnson on the job. We'll need plans drawn up. And that construction mob need notifying too, now that the job is twice the size."

"On it, mate," Marshall said. "Oh and Cal ..."

"Yeah?"

"Best break the news gently."

Callan's gaze swung my way, and the smile slipped off his face. "Gotcha."

They terminated the call. My hands were clammier

than before, and my heart heavier than it had been for a long while as I sat there waiting for Callan to tell me what had him practically peeing his pants with excitement. Chewing on the corner of my lip, I remained focused on the road.

"We're buying the land by the creek for Bellevue's expansions."

Coldness gripped me as the vision of my mother's tears, the unpaid bills, her assurance we'd find the money to upgrade the motel, all assaulted my visual memory. This had happened before.

Pop's land.

His legacy ...

The last little bit left.

She couldn't. My stomach turned over. That was *my* creek. Pop had said it was to be passed down and Callan ... Callan ...

"That's my land. She can't sell it."

"You sure? Because the papers are practically signed."

I couldn't look at him right now.

And Mum. How could she do that to me, to us? That land was in her keeping until I reached twenty-five. How in the hell could she even sell it? Surely, there were laws preventing it.

My hand thumped into my chest, right over the tightness around my heart. Pop loved that place so much, and we'd spent so many hours together there when I was growing up that it almost felt as if I were losing him all over again.

FOURTEEN

Driving into Armidale felt different than it had any other time during the entire three years I'd lived here. My heart and thoughts raced. The closer we got, the more my feet tapped against the floor of Callan's huge truck. I glanced out the back window for the millionth time and sure enough, Logan's Corolla trailed behind us.

"So, this is your college town?"

I drummed my fingers on my knee. "Uh-huh."

"Vet Science, yeah?"

"Mmm."

"Molly," Callan said. "Talk to me."

"My mother sold our land to Marshall. He's been wanting if for years anyway. There's nothing to say."

He pulled the car over to the curb and cut the engine. I kept my eyes on the front windscreen while the red Corolla sped past. After staring at me so long I thought my ears might catch fire, Callan shuffled in his seat and turned over the engine. "Are you at least going to tell me where to go?"

I sure felt like telling him exactly where to go, but instead of being rude, I said, "Take a left here, then it's the first right just up the other side of the hill."

He followed my directions and the second the stupid oversized truck stopped next to Logan's little car, I threw open the door and jumped down. The engine died behind me and I scrubbed shaky hands over my tired eyes. Marshall and Mum and Callan, too. How long had they all been conspiring to steal my land?

The screen door flew open.

"You're here!" Savvy barrelled toward me, her arms extended, and her blonde hair swished around her pretty face. "I missed you so much."

Weariness overtook me as I leaned into my friend. "Me too."

"It's only been a month." Always the voice of reason, Liv scooped me and Savvy into a group hug.

"Who's the hottie?" Of course, it only took Savvy half a heartbeat to notice Callan. "Have you been holding out on us, Molly?"

I shrugged off her arm and ignored Liv's questioning look. It didn't last long anyway; politeness got the better of my socialite friend and she stepped forward, hand extended. "I'm Olivia, and you must be Callan."

"That's me."

Savvy looked from me to him, him to me, but I spun her around with a question. "How's Dane coping since his dad ... you know?" I wasn't quite sure how to say died.

She sighed. "Bottling up his grief. He misses his dad all the time, but he's trying to hold it together for his mum."

"That's got to be hard."

She nodded, steering me off the driveway and through the front door. As we entered the tiny kitchen, she glanced behind us then whispered, "What's with Mr Tall, Dark and Handsome?"

"Nothing."

Savvy planted her palms around my shoulders and ducked a little to catch my downturned gaze. I followed her eyes as she pulled herself up to normal height, and I repeated, "Nothing."

She raised a brow.

"Honestly, nothing."

"I don't buy it."

"Just through this way." Liv's voice interrupted our painful non-conversation as she and Callan appeared in the kitchen. She extracted a glass from the cupboard above the sink and poured water into it, then handed him the full glass.

Callan's eyes swung to me, and I met his stare.

"Where are you from, Callan?" Liv said, but Savvy cleared her throat, pulling the other girl's attention back her way.

"Gold Coast, but more recently, Bindarra Creek." He never broke our eye contact.

"Nice," Liv answered. "Help yourself to whatever you'd like to eat and drink."

Then she disappeared into the living room, pulled away by Savvy, and it was just me and him again, pinned together by a long, hard stare.

"Molly." He sighed. "We thought it was your mother's land, and she was happy to sell. She's all but signed the papers." He reached for me, but I stepped back. "We're not going to rip up the spot. It's bloody beautiful down there. With a couple of condos to pull in the family crowd—"

"Holy freaking ..." Condos. Huge, manmade structures. "*No*."

I pulled one of Savvy's Vodka Cruisers out of the fridge—I'd have to owe her—and followed the sound of my friends' voices to where they sat in the backyard. Taking the empty seat beside Savvy, I clinked my bottle against hers and said, "Thanks."

My friends chattered as they sat around the outdoor table where Liv was perched on Logan's knee, and Savvy glanced at her phone every few seconds. Jordan seemed to have disappeared, no doubt off to work.

It took a while for Callan to wander outside too, but when he did, I downed the remainder of my raspberry drink and set the empty bottle on the table. A fresh one found its way into my hand, and sitting around the barbeque, Callan became the new play toy, answering a barrage of questions the girls threw at him. Sitting at the opposite side of the table, with his boot cocked up on his knee, he dished out plenty of sexy smiles.

The pile of empties in the centre of the table grew, and if I wasn't careful I'd drink Savvy dry. Perhaps a run to the bottle shop was in order. I opened my mouth to say as much, but both my friends were looking at Callan as if he were the Pied bloody Piper. Either that or Don Juan. Even Logan was enthralled by whatever stupid story Callan was spinning. Tossing back the last of my drink, I clinked the bottle onto the table with its brothers.

"Mind if I indulge again?"

"No worries, hon." Savvy offered up a smile as she

leaned in to whisper, "Problems in paradise?"

My gaze slid to the man who'd just told me he was developing *my* creek. "There is no paradise."

She grimaced as she sipped at her drink. And after a few moments, Liv appeared from inside carrying cleaning gear, which she passed off to Logan at the barbeque, coupled with a kiss to his jaw. Logan's arm swooped around her, and pulling Liv flush against his body, he kissed her as if the rest of us weren't watching. I had no idea when either of the loved-up pair had moved from their earlier seat, but clearly it was getting close to dinner time. Leaving her boyfriend at the grill, Liv waltzed toward us, suggestively wriggling her eyebrows at Savvy.

"Dane's here!" Savvy shot up off her chair and raced toward the small unit. The back door flew against the wall and slapped back into place as she hurled herself through it and disappeared from sight.

Callan glanced away from our stare down when a shrill squeal cut through the air. Liv continued bustling around us, stopping when Logan's hand pulled her back to him for a second not-for-company kiss, and that was enough. I shoved my chair back, needing to get the hell away from Callan, from this couple-filled love-nest. Barrelling through the back door, and making for the fridge again, I tugged the door open. As the cool air snaked around my bare legs, the presence of another person crowded the room. So help me God, if it was—

"Molly ..."

I spun around, fire burning in my chest. "Leave me alone, Callan."

He removed the stupid black hat from his head, and turned the brim in his thick fingers. "I didn't mean to hurt you."

"What? When you made plans to ruin the one place I care about? The property my grandfather left to me in trust?"

His eyes rounded.

"If my mother sells it, there's nothing I can do." My shoulder slammed his as I pushed past his bulky frame blocking the doorway. "When she said you were trouble I should have listened."

"That's bullshit."

"The hell it is." I needed out, needed away, but he kept following me, from the kitchen to the living room and back to the kitchen. I pushed past him again, determined to get some space, but Callan grabbed my shoulder, forcing me to face him. Anger clouded his face, but I couldn't care less. I had nothing more to say to him. N-O-T-H-I-N-G. Nothing.

"If I told you how cute you are all riled up—"

"Leave me the fuck alone." I shoved through the front door.

"Molly ..."

Ignoring him, I passed Savvy and Dane making out by his new car. The back of my throat burned. A firm grip caught my shoulder and spun me around. Callan's mouth worked, but hearing what he had to say wasn't even on my give-a-crap radar.

"I told you to fuck off."

I strode down the street, blocking out the shocked look on Dane's face, probably due to my colourful language.

I tugged my phone out of my pocket and dialled.

"Akuna Motel, good evening." My mother's voice filled the line.

"Is it true?"

"Molly?"

"Are you selling the last of Pop's estate?"

She huffed, and rattling papers were the only other sound coming from her end of the line.

"After you already sold off the house and stables the second he died to fund your motel dream?" I scoffed. "Nice one, Mum."

"That land is mine."

"No, Molly it isn't. It was left to me to administer, for our family."

"Until I turn twenty-five."

I hit *end call* and lucky for me, the bottle-O wasn't too far from Logan's apartment. Screw my savings. I needed a Sambuca night.

The cashier slammed the till shut as I walked in. "Make it fast. We shut in five minutes."

I went straight to the back wall where this place kept its spirits and plucked a seven hundred ml bottle of the black stuff right off the shelf without even looking at the price tag. This guy wanted to get off work and go party? Well, I wasn't about to hold him up.

Almost fifty bucks later, I walked out of the tiny bottle shop, brown paper bag in hand. When Jordan got home from work, he'd do shots with me. Screw being the fifth wheel and watching all the happy couples share midnight kisses. I'd clink glasses with J instead.

FIFTEEN

On New Year's day God smote me with another hangover. And a car ride back to Bindarra Creek with one of the three people I didn't want to see, let alone be cooped up with. Asking Logan or even Dane to run me home would have been utterly selfish, so I sucked it up and prepared to ignore the hell out of *him*. Even though it was Mum's and Marshall's doing, and lashing out at Callan was probably wrong, tamping down the anger was damn impossible.

Liv gave me one of her tight goodbye hugs, and as we pulled apart she pressed a bottle of water and a foil packet into my hand. "For your headache."

I frowned, and she said, "After the way you were drinking last night, I know you have one."

I had another hazy memory, too, but this time I knew I hadn't slept with anyone. Still, I'd rather not recall the stroke of midnight. Last night didn't exactly top my list of best New Year's Eves.

Savvy swooped in, tossing one arm over Liv's

shoulders and the other around my waist. "Girl, you have to keep us in the loop. Whatever's going down, we're here. Hell knows you've been there for me often enough."

"Me too," Liv said.

"And that shirt ..." Savvy waved her hand at my faded Minnie Mouse number. "It's got to go."

Olivia scowled at Sav, and I smiled. "I love you girls."

"You too." Liv kissed my cheek. "Now, take care."

I climbed up into the truck where Callan already sat, his hands on the wheel. "You ready?"

"Yup." I pushed the painkillers out of their package and popped them into my mouth, then guzzled down half the water.

As we reversed out of the drive, Savvy held a hand to her ear, pinkie finger and thumb extended in a 'call me' sign. Yeah, I still didn't feel like talking, but I blew her a kiss then dropped my head against the window, closing my eyes. Sleep didn't come quickly or easily. It was a damn shame really, but faking it meant Callan didn't try to talk, and that made life easier. Well, until nausea churned up my stomach. Darn motion sickness. Or maybe it was the hangover. Eventually, I peeked at the road to prevent barfing. If Callan noticed, he didn't take the opportunity to speak.

Mum was supposed to have my best interest at heart. She was supposed to care about her own father's wishes, but no. The hollow ache moved from my stomach to my chest, and I closed my eyes again. This time sleep must have taken over, because I dreamt.

Hot fingers pushed into my hair, messaging my scalp. I moaned against the warmth of Callan's mouth, desire curling low in my belly. This guy sure knew how to kiss. Using the leg hooked behind his back, I flipped us over and arched my back as he sat up, cradling my body against his. As if he could sense the change in me, his hips ground against mine and he kissed me like he meant to do more than just kiss. My hands dipped under the band of his jeans, my thumb brushing against the hair trailing down from his navel, and I pushed at the denim. Taking the hint, he fidgeted beneath me, slipped the jeans off—

Need owned me. I needed to feel Callan's skin against my own. Needed to skate my tongue over his top lip. Needed to feel connected to him in every possible way. With my lips, my hands, my thighs—

My eyes shot open. Dark orbs the colour of storm clouds stared back, and heat rushed my face. I swallowed against the dryness in my mouth and blinked.

"We're home," Callan said gently. His lips, so full and kissable, hovered only a hairsbreadth from my face.

I inhaled shakily and he moved closer, his breath dusting my lips. My eyes dropped closed and everything felt right until ... the creek. Feeling intoxicated all over again, I reached for the car door, my head fuzzy. I pushed past him and pain shot through my face as my nose smashed his chin. That didn't stop me from stepping out of the truck and climbing down. Holding my aching nose, I slammed the door closed before he could say something arrogant, and pushed through the Akuna's front entrance without a backward glance. Thankfully Dad was at the front desk and not Mum. I was in no mood to listen to one of her lectures right then. Scratch that. I was in no mood to see her face, period.

"Hi, honey."

"Did you know about Mum selling the last of Bellevue?"

His expression hardened with a clenching jaw. "She didn't make the decision lightly."

"It wasn't anyone's decision," I shouted, "but mine. Pop wanted—"

"Molly, don't—"

I ducked my head and raced up the stairs, not feeling like talking to anyone. He hadn't wanted me to buy paint with my hard-earned money, yet he was fine with taking my creek without asking.

I burst through the door and from her spot sitting in front of the TV, my mother glanced up, but returned her attention to the medical soap quicker than it took me to cross the room. Anger curled inside my chest at the way she'd thrown away Pop's property like it meant nothing when it should have been the exact opposite. Her parents had spent a lifetime building that business on land that had been passed down for generations, and now it was no more, destined for some huge enterprise that would bulldoze the lot. Instead of passed on to me, who would have cherished it.

"I hate you." The shout tore my throat open. "How could you sell it?"

Mum swivelled, looking over the back of the couch. "The money will fix up the motel so we can support this family. What point is land that we have no use for? The rates are just another bill."

I screamed so loud my throat burned.

"That land was left to me, Molly, to oversee until

such time—"

"I didn't mean legally, dammit." Flinging my bedroom door opened, I tossed my backpack into the corner of my room and picked up the photo frame on my desk then sunk onto my bed, cocooned by teddy bears. Created from rustic timber, Pop and I had made it together years ago. He'd stolen the glass out of one of Grandma's old frames and the photo ... I smoothed a thumb over the image of his face. Over the huge grin he sported, while tucked under his giant arm, seven-year-old me held up the catfish we'd caught together. That was the day he'd taught me how to hook my own bait.

My throat burned as tears slid down my cheeks and splashed against the glass.

How could she?

SIXTEEN

The buzz of my phone vibrating against the desk woke me at stupid o'clock. Stupid because getting out of bed when it was still partly dark was only for the insane. Apparently that included me. I hauled myself upright and reached for the offending device, jamming my thumb into the power button to shut it up. Sitting on my bed for a few moments didn't help pull myself into wakefulness, so giving up, I fished around the pile of clothes hanging over the back of my chair, and in the half-light of dawn found my jeans. I pulled them and a T-shirt on, then slid my feet into my Docs. It only took ten minutes to gulp down a glass of water and grab an apple for the road.

I tossed my bag into the back seat, and in no time passed Bellevue farmhouse, the pink hues of dawn reflecting off her white walls. As much as I loathed crawling out of bed at the butt crack of dawn there was something serene about this time of day, as if all the worries, all the problems in the world, ceased to exist. At dawn, it was as if mankind were back in Adam and Eve's Eden with not a care in the world.

But like that sanctuary, mine too would soon change.

I swung the old Ford into her spot under the ghostly white giant, and climbed out, careful not to slam the door. Noise travelled when the rest of the world was asleep, and I really didn't want to draw the attention of anyone in the house. I always said stuff I shouldn't when my heart hurt.

The horses were a different story. These big, strong creatures were far more loveable than most people. Jed's huge head hung over the gate of his stall, his liquid gaze following my movement along the wide hall. Stopping, I gave his nose a rub and scratched under his chin. "Smells kind of musty in here, old boy."

I hadn't bothered getting my bag out of the car. I wasn't planning on hanging around longer than it took to finish up my duties, so whether it was habit or intuition that made me hit the office first I couldn't be certain. Marshall had dug into sorting the place out over the past few weeks, so now the usually cluttered room practically sparkled with cleanliness. A brand new laptop sat on the desk beside a blank notepad. Plus, a filing cabinet I'd never before seen filled the back corner of the room. What caught my eye, though, was the cardboard box pushed to the side of the old oak desk. Sealed with packaging tape, my name covered one whole side in massive bold lettering.

Well, that was new.

Picking at the tape didn't lift it, so I hooked the keys out of my pocket and pushed one under the side.

The serrated edge cut through the plastic and the lid popped open. Pulling it back, I peered inside and my throat clogged up. The picture of Pop and I that had been on the noticeboard since he'd held me up to pin it in place rested on top of a box full of papers. Probably things that had belonged to my grandfather.

One of the ponies snorted out in the stables, pulling me back to the task at hand:

- Get in
- Get it done
- Get out before anyone showed up

Exploring this box would have to wait. Taking a last look at the picture, I pushed the lid closed and hit the store room. I wouldn't mind running into Marshall. I had a whole bag of questions for the man who'd been my friend for years. Like 'Why did you pressure her into selling when you already have so much?'

Of course, I knew the answer to that: expansion. Every damn resident in Bindarra Creek was trying to drive more business into town and that wasn't really a bad thing. But it didn't stop the hurt twisting me up.

Prepping the horses' breakfast and getting it into the troughs took all of fifteen minutes. Shovelling dirty straw out of the stables took much longer and by the time I'd finished, they had too, so I clipped a lead on Jed and another on Angel, then led them both to the east paddock. It was still a bit of a mess from the mud run, but the ditches were filled in and these horses needed the exercise.

Unclipping the lead from Jed's halter, I gave him a slap on the rump and ordered him to have a good day. Angel, too.

By the time I returned to the office it must have

been close to nine a.m.—long past time to hit the road. I scooped my box off the desk, and cradling its weight under my arm, got out of there. My foot clipped a boot and I stumbled into a firm body. A steadying hand around my waist pulled me upright, and before glancing up, I knew that it was him. There was something about his presence that thickened the air in the room.

If I had been paying more attention to what was in front of me and less to the box in my hands, I would've seen him in time. Squaring my shoulders, I reshuffled the weight of my load and mumbled, "Thanks."

"My pleasure."

Shaking off the ridiculous desire leaching through me—I was angry with him, damn it—I walked away. Exiting the stables twisted my heart in the craziest of ways, and it felt like something inside me was about to snap in half. That was probably why, as I set the box onto the passenger seat of my borrowed car, I glanced back at the timber-plank building.

With his shoulder propped against the doorframe, Callan had his hat in his hand hanging loosely by his thigh while he watched me. Our gazes caught and held. If words could travel over space without sound, then they did in that moment. Everything about his look said he was sorry, but that didn't undo what he'd been a part of. Tearing my gaze away, I slammed the door and forced myself to walk around to the other side of the car and get in. The scorching air inside the car seared my throat as I took a breath, so I wound the window down, then leaned across to the other side and worked the handle at a funny angle to get a bit of air flow.

I started the engine, pausing with my hands on the wheel. My eyes dropped closed, and I drew in a deep breath. He knew how special the creek was to me. Another hot inhale filled my lungs.

He was still there, in my rear-vision mirror, as I drove away. Warm wind whipped through the car, stinging my eyes with its heat. They certainly weren't stinging because I wanted to cry. My shoulders slumped, my heart sunk, and my temples throbbed. Why did it feel as if I were the one in the wrong? The weariness of being sad overwhelmed me on the drive home, and pulling up at the Akuna, I reached across to delve into the cardboard box.

Sometimes it felt like yesterday that I'd baked beside Grandma in the kitchen and mucked out stalls with Pop, then other times it felt like every day during the five years since his heart attack had lasted far more than its worth. I placed the photo on the dash and fished out the plaque that had always sat on the huge oak desk. Engraved on the front were the words, *open for business*. On the reverse, *gone fishing*. It was so very him.

Sweat beaded on my neck and trickled down the opening of my shirt while I extracted knick-knacks and other stuff from the box. It wasn't until the thing was almost empty that my fingers closed around a bunch of files. The first folder held a heap of loose papers that looked like some kind of hand-drawn plans. So old they were brittle and yellow, they seemed to be for the farmhouse, only it looked much smaller than it should have been. Another wad of folded papers sat behind the first, so I opened the one on top, only to find more plans. These ones were of the same building, including what I'd never realised were extensions. A new kitchen, an outbuilding that Pop had used as a work shed. The plans continued, each new set less frail than the last, until finally, the last papers contained blueprints for the stables with instantly recognisable handwriting. It was surprising that Marshall didn't want to keep these, but he probably had updated plans on file. I swiped a hand across my sweaty forehead and, carefully placing all the papers back inside the manila folder, I reached for the final item in the cardboard box. Getting out of the rapidly warming car probably should have rated some importance, but the moment my gaze caught on the second folder, I wasn't moving. A fat A4 envelope peeked out the top, my name scrawled on the front in Pop's sloping handwriting. Curious, I flipped it over to the sealed back and slid my finger under the flap. It didn't come free with a gentle pull, so I tore that sucker open and reached inside. Another, smaller envelope toppled out with a book that looked like a glossy black and white magazine.

My sweet Molly.

My heart squeezed at the slanting words on the envelope that sometime, someplace, Pop had penned me. Between this morning's clash with Callan and the unboxing of all these memories, surely I was about to melt from the heart outwards.

My glistening arms certainly made it look as if I were.

Setting the letter on my lap, I took a closer look at the book. Titled *Bindarra Creek High, Class of '96*, it had to be my mother's yearbook. Fun.

After pocketing the car keys and tossing everything back into the box, I placed the letter and photo on top then climbed out of the car, book in hand. Leaning against the white vehicle, I flicked open the book's front page and found a bunch of signatures and well wishes. Mum must have had plenty of friends, because the entire inside cover was crowded and words overflowed onto the next page. Only someone had taken to the messages with a Sharpie. Entire sections had been completely blacked out. I flipped through the pages, glancing at all the black-and-white photos, searching for her familiar face or maybe Dad's, since they'd been high school sweethearts and were in the same grade. It didn't take long to find an image. Only a few pages in was one of the two of them sitting on a bench that still graced the school's quad. Both were so baby-faced, and they weren't alone. Another guy sat between them—the school uniform and muscled legs a dead giveaway of his sex, unlike his face, for that too had been blacked out. As had the caption underneath. With his arm wrapped across Mum's shoulders and her looking all gooey-eyed at him, Dad watched on from her other side, his usual smile absent. Most probably because his mate was hitting on his girl.

I flicked through a few more pages and found the three of them again. The caption was defaced and the same bloke had been scratched out of the picture. Once again Dad was on the outer, while the other two held hands, this time wearing formalwear as if they were dressed for the traditional end-of-year dance. I'd always thought my parents were each other's first love. This sure looked like a different story though.

She must have moved straight from that guy onto Dad.

Kicking the car door closed and walking into the

office, I slapped the yearbook onto the counter where Mum sat. "Marshall found this."

She glanced up, looked to the book, and all colour drained from her face. "Where did he find that?"

"In Pop's old office." I pushed it farther toward her. "Nice hair, by the way."

She shuddered, and looking at the book as if it were a live Redback spider, she didn't move. *Whatever.* I had bigger issues at hand. Like the letter from my grandfather.

"I'll tell Marshall you said thanks." I trotted up the stairs and once inside, dropped the box onto my desk then pulled out the second envelope. Beds were created to be flopped on, so I shoved off all the old teddy bears and fell back onto the soft mattress and slid a finger under the sealed flap. This envelope opened far easier than the last and was far slimmer, with only a single sheet of paper inside.

Not sure whether to smile or cry, I slid the parchment out and opened it up.

My dearest Molly

Tears flooded my vision at the sight of not my pop's handwriting, but my gran's. He must have sealed it away for her. I pulled up the hem on my T-shirt and wiped the tears away.

You are the biggest joy of my life and that of your grandfather's, too. Know that we both love you a great deal and hold your heart close to ours. I suspect your home life hasn't been warm, but I hope that we've given you, our beloved granddaughter, what our daughter could not.

I can't go to my grave without telling you that it was never my choice not to tell you the truth. Now that your mother has explained all, my hope is that reading my words will remind you of how very loved you are and always have been. You are a true treasure.

David is a wonderful man. Allowing him to help raise you was one of the best choices Patricia ever made. Try to understand that your mother's lack of compassion comes not from a place of hatred, but rather one of fear.

With much love,
Grandma
XXX

What in the *what?* I read it through again, but the words still didn't make a lot of sense. Of course Grandma loved me. That bit was unmistakable, but secrets and truth and *allowing* Dad to raise me? I grabbed hold of my head as if that would stop it spinning.

Allowing ...

Secrets ...

Truth ...

I couldn't even begin to figure out what it all meant.

Gathering up the paper, I traipsed downstairs to where my mother still sat, staring at that stupid yearbook as if it were going to jump right up and attack her.

The boy in the pictures ...

I was born in '97.

"Mum." She looked up, her dark eyes almost vacant as they met mine. "Is there something you need to tell me?"

The deepest frown creased her forehead, and my

usually composed mother crumpled before my very eyes. I should have walked around the desk and hugged her, but I was too busy reaching in to reach out.

I snatched the book up off the counter and flicked to one of the images I'd seen earlier. My parents were young when they'd had me. Only—I counted backward twenty years—she was nineteen when I was born. That meant I must have been conceived when Mum was in grade twelve. Oh my ...

On a shaky voice, I asked, "Is Dad my real dad?"

She didn't respond. The tears that trickled down her red cheeks were answer enough.

SEVENTEEN

My mother looked up at me, stony as an ice-sculpted gargoyle, her lips sealed.

"Is Dad my real father?" I repeated.

She glanced toward the door, pushed the book away, and swiped the silent tears off her cheeks.

"Are you going to answer me?"

"It's not ..." she choked out a sob, "... a pretty story."

"Not a pretty story?" My arms shook as I wrapped them around myself. "Spare me, Mum."

After several moments of cold silence, she returned her attention to the bookings sheet. I shook my head and spun around. The exit to this place had never looked more inviting. Shoving the door open, I stalked outside and walked straight to my car. The car door creaked as it opened, and I threw myself behind the wheel with anger thrumming through my fingers and sorrow beating at my heart.

The engine spluttered and coughed, then died.

Dammit. Trying again, I pushed the clutch to the floor and turned the key. Nothing.

The wheel made a good punching bag for my fisted hands. If it didn't start this time, walking would have to do. I'd probably flooded the stupid engine. Sending up a prayer to the God my mother swore existed, I twisted the key in the ignition and waited, listening. The old beast shuddered. Shuddered ... and the darn thing finally kicked over. *Thank you, God.*

Screw letting her idle so she didn't stall. The wheels spun as I reversed out of the parking space. Dad glanced up from where he was washing down the picket fence out front, but I didn't stop. The basher took a wide turn out onto Mount Ingalls Road, and with my shoulders set, I stared down the stupid freaking cenotaph. There was no logical reason to be so damn scared of a hunk of cement. With my jaw clenched so tight my teeth ached, I drove straight at the soldier, and swerved to circle around him, indicating at the last minute that I'd turn off to the right—up Main Street. But I didn't get off that damn circle. I couldn't go back to Bellevue or to my sanctuary at the creek when there was no guarantee of solitude. Lapping the soldier once, twice, and a third time, I finally exited, going back the way I'd come. Mount Ingalls Road led to Armidale. Speeding past the motel, I kept the old car working hard until we were well out of town.

Laying off the gas, I looked down at the fuel gauge. It had less than an eighth of a tank. Well, crap. That wouldn't get me much farther than back the distance I'd come.

Pulling over to the road's shoulder, I cut the engine and slumped back in the seat, pressing my hand against my eyes. Bloody typical that whatever could go against me would. Geez, this whole situation was worse than a freaking soap opera. Maybe I should contact Dr Phil or Jerry Springer.

Sighing, I dropped my hand, opened my eyes and looked at the huge mountain looming in the distance. Its flat top reminded me of the old rumour that used to float around school. Apparently Eagle Rock contained a hidden cave, one that had been used as a hideout by bushrangers back in the day. Of course, no one had ever found it.

I grabbed my backpack from the back seat and slung it over my shoulders, then locked up the old basher.

Shoving a foot on the wire fence beside the road, I climbed up and over, careful not to snag myself on the barbs, then jumped down into the long grass below.

The first kilometre was easy walking. Through a paddock filled with thirsty-looking lucerne that belonged to the Sullivans, the incline didn't really start until I reached the edge of the paddock, and even then it was gradual. For twenty years, everyone had let me live a lie. Why? The skeleton lurking in our family closest was one damn ugly sucker.

And Mum was cold, according to her own mother? Sure she didn't like hugs, but cold? Seriously, Grandma. She was just Mum, and that was what all mums were like, weren't they? Not that I'd had a lot to do with other people's mothers, but my friends all talked about their parents and Liv's mum sure didn't sound like a hugger.

My lungs opened from the steady pace as I started the climb up the snaking toes of Mount Ingalls. The base of the giant mountain sloped steadily upward, the hill only sparsely spotted with vegetation. It wasn't until the incline turned suddenly steeper that the forest grew denser, and I found myself fighting against lantana, fallen branches, and bracken almost taller than my waist. I stopped for a breather, pulling out my bottle of water. Maybe hitting the bush without a compass and map wasn't such a good idea. But I knew these mountains like I knew the creek. I'd practically grown up bashing through the scrub with ... *not my father.* A sharp pain twisted inside my chest. Had he lived a lie, too?

Why ...?

Why?

"Why?" My scream echoed through the air, bouncing back over and over. I shoved the water bottle into my bag and hefted it over my shoulder, then with renewed vigour made for the rocky outcropping right ahead. The centre was almost like a sheer cliff, if only a few metres tall, so I picked a path off to the left where boulders were interspersed with fallen twigs and leaf-covered ground. Stepping up onto the lowest rock, I used my hands to help heave me up to the next, then walked an unsteady path to the top landing.

There are always lots of sounds in the bush—the call of native birds, scrub turkeys scratching up the forest floor, and the wind howling through the trees, but only one sound could freeze me to the spot.

Render me immobile.

Hissing, the hugest Brown snake I'd ever seen slithered over the sunny outcropping. Holy freaking hell. My heart thrashed against its confines and my body jerked awake. Back-pedalling a few steps nice and fast, my foot slipped on a loose stone and I toppled off balance, my palms scraping along the dirt, trying to find purchase.

I fell, tumbled butt over boob with rocks grazing my shoulders, my thighs, my knees.

My left ankle slammed into a boulder, and the weight of my body crashed into my bent leg. Something cracked. If the snake was still there, I couldn't see it. That didn't stop my heart hammering, as if the slithery reptile had chased me down the cliff. It could have for all I knew. Browns were deadly. If it struck, there'd be no getting to hospital for anti-venom from out here. I'd be lucky to make it back to the car.

Heat prickled my skin, and I pushed myself up to get the hell out of there, but pain shot through my ankle before I'd even settled my weight on it. Peering into the undergrowth, I searched for the snake, my heart beating up a storm. It was like searching for a grain of salt in a bag of sand. With branches, twigs and leaves—all the same colour as the venomous Brown—littering the ground, there was no way to be sure where the creature was or was not.

I pushed up onto my knees then raised myself onto my good foot. Tentatively placing the gummy one on the ground, I went to take a step and crumpled into the dirt, my hands flying to cradle my screaming limb. Tears prickled my eyes and all thoughts of the snake evaporated as I sat there in the middle of the bush, holding my ankle.

Sometimes life sucked.

That didn't mean I had to accept it.

Getting up was easier the third time, since I knew just where not to place any pressure. With a palm pressed against the rough trunk of an Iron Bark, I hopped forward on my good foot. The jar sent pain spearing through my other foot and up into my leg, but there was no choice. I had to get back to the basher. I hopped again, this time with no support for my hands. Sucking back the tears, I kept going. *Hop. Hop. Hop.*

My foot caught, spinning me off balance, and an arm thrown up at the last minute was the only thing that saved my face from slamming into the stick-covered ground.

I should have been too proud to call for help—heck knew, I was still too angry—but sometimes a girl had to suck the bad stuff up and admit she wasn't Wonder Woman. Getting out of here on my own wasn't going to happen.

Lying on the ground, I twisted myself around to extract my phone from the front pocket of my backpack and scrolled through the recent calls, right past Akuna, past Bellevue, and past Marshall. I stopped at the person who I knew would come to help me without judgement.

Dad's phone rang and rang and rang.

I rolled onto my back, ignoring the sharp sting of a stick stabbing my butt, and held my breath, trying not to cry at the pain.

"Molly?"

"Callan?"

Just freaking great. Drawing a breath through the stupid lump blocking my throat stung, but I wouldn't cry. What the frig was he doing answering my dad's mobile phone? Why was he even in the same place? I pulled myself up into a sitting position and sucked in a sharp breath, then exhaled on a whimper as my foot throbbed worse than it had at the mud run.

"What's wrong, babe?"

"I'm not your ..." I didn't have the will left to even finish that stupid sentence.

"Something's wrong. Where in the hell are you?"

"Is Dad there?"

"Where are you?" Callan's words were firm.

"At the base of Mount Ingalls. Just off the Sullivan property ... there's a field full of lucerne."

"On my way."

Looking at the phone which showed Marshall's name instead of Dad's, I fell back against the dusty ground, my ankle throbbing as if it had its own oversized heartbeat. These last few days had issued blow after blow and here I was at the edge of the Akuna National Park, ready to hike up the largest mountain in the area without any preparation.

Callan was right. Running away was what I did best.

EIGHTEEN

Getting up again, I forced myself to hobble on the ankle from hell. My steps may have been completely unsteady, taken a full five minutes each, and hurt like hell, but I put one heel in front of the next foot and kept going. By the time I reached the clearing, my sore foot wouldn't move at all, and I was back to hopping.

My phone pinged out a polyphonic tune, and digging it from my pocket, I picked up.

"Mol, it's a helluva big paddock. Where are you?"

"Toward the middle, in the bush. I'm—" A shaky breath hissed between my teeth. "Almost to the edge."

"Hold on. I'm just about there."

Just as the trees began thinning, a distant shout tickled the air, and muffled, it came down the line too.

Gritting my teeth, I stilled, my weary good leg aching from overuse. The noise came again, this time a little clearer.

"I can hear you," I said into the phone, then dropping it, cupped my hands around my mouth and yelled, "Cooee."

"Molly!" Callan's shout cut through the warm afternoon before I'd raised the mobile to my ear.

"Cooee," I called again, using the bushman's ancient call.

My leg ached so much it buckled, and I caught myself from falling by planting my hands on the ground and slowly lowering myself. I probably could have shuffled along on my knees, but exhaustion had set in. Callan continued telling me to hold on, and I kept shouting toward the field, until finally, his black hat and strong frame powered out of the lucerne crop.

Tears threatened to break through again, but I gulped those suckers down.

I hit the hang up button on my phone. It felt like a lifetime between when I saw him and when he reached me, sweat sticking the front of his T-shirt to his chest. He dropped to his haunches, his hand brushing over my cheek. I soaked in his soft and caring gaze, then drank in the rest of him with my eyes. Touching my arm, which stung like all buggery, his fingers probed as he assessed my injuries. Finally, Callan gently lifted my left foot. Pain sliced through the muscle, cutting right up my thigh and pounding into my hip. The metallic taste of blood coated my tongue as my teeth bit down against the torture.

"Baby," Callan whispered by my ear. "I'm gonna lift you up."

Strong arms scooped me off the ground, the pain beating against my leg unrelenting as the firmness of his chest met my curled body. My vision clouded with red, the agony swallowing everything else as he started moving.

"Shh." His lips stirred against my forehead. "We're going to get you out of here, alright?"

He kept talking as we moved, but my eyes stayed closed, my focus turned inward, on keeping the hurt at bay.

"You're amazing, Molly." Callan's voice rumbled against my cheek as he held me. "You care for the horses like they're all yours. You look after the stables better than even Marshall can. But your kindness isn't even your best trait. You're strong, baby. So strong."

The hurt ebbed, flowed, but the thumping ache remained constant.

"You don't put up with anyone's shit," he continued. "And I love that. You didn't put up with Callie-May that night I first met you." He chuckled. "To see that chick stumble over her own insults ... bloody priceless. And beautiful, Molly. You're more gorgeous than any of those uptight chicks. You don't give a damn what anyone thinks and hell, that's a rare gem. Those huge eyes of yours ..."

I felt a smile touch my lips through the grimace. My eyes rolled back. This pain ...

Pain ...

Pain.

A soft pressure brushed the crown of my head. "Mol, are you still with me?"

"Mmm. Here." I forced my eyes open, focusing on his face.

"I need your help to get through this fence. I'm gonna set you on the ground."

Bending, he held me close to his chest until the long grass brushed against my cheek. He placed me flat on my back on the ground, and hooking a hand around the bottom rung of wire, Callan stretched it up almost to the next strand.

"Roll, baby."

My foggy brain didn't understand.

"Roll under the fence. It'll hurt less than climbing."

"Mmhmm."

Bracing myself with a stiff leg, I tilted onto my side, then over onto my tummy. Grass tickled my face and a rock dug into my boob, but it held nothing to the fire burning in my foot.

"Almost there," Callan urged.

I rolled up onto my other shoulder and my ankle bumped the ground.

Holy freaking hell.

A thud landed beside me, and Callan's face appeared right near mine. "I'm here." He scooped me up into his strong arms, and nestled against him, I somehow felt a little comfort. A few more steps and he settled me into the front of his truck, then jumped up into the driver's side and spun the car around.

Gritting my teeth, I sucked in sharp breath after breath. My eyes scrunched closed as we drove. Red and hazy, the back of my eyelids throbbed in time with my foot, my heart. Every damn thing beat, and each dip in the road jarred my whole body, starting the pain afresh.

The drive took forever.

"I'm sorry." Callan's words broke through the fog of pain "If you don't want to sell the creek perhaps we can find a way to stop them."

Frowning at how close he sounded and the feel of hands sliding underneath me, I said, "You'd do that?"

"It's important to you."

He slid me out of the car, and my head dropped into the warmth of his chest and Callan shuffled my weight, his whole frame jolting as a doorbell chimed.

"That Molly McLean?" a female voice asked.

"Yep. She's in a shit-load of pain from a busted ankle."

"Lucky it's been a quiet afternoon. Bring her straight through."

I faded in and out while someone poked and prodded. At some point I was moved to a wheelchair and pushed into another room for X-rays, soon followed by a handful of painkillers, which stripped me of the pain, replacing it with a tiredness that I couldn't fight.

Consciousness floated back. The steady hum of a radio created background noise against the buzz of voices that weren't close by. Lifting heavy eyelids, my fuzzy vision cleared and Callan still sat by my side. His fingers had found their way into mine. He issued a reassuring squeeze, and I tried to smile, but my face was too elastic.

"Molly." My gaze slipped to the other side of the bed, where Bindarra Creek's ancient doctor regarded me. "It appears that you have a fracture of the tibia. It's a nice clean break, so we're going to boot the foot up, which should help you keep the injury immobile while the bone knits. That will need to stay in place for a few weeks, but once it comes off absolutely no weight bearing on that foot for six weeks."

I nodded.

"Mr Hunter here tells me this foot has a history."

"It was sprained last time."

"There's nothing on your records."

"It wasn't that bad. I didn't come in to the polyclinic."

"I see. Well, you've got a weakness there, which more than likely contributed to this break. You'll need to take care of it in future."

I glanced down at the rogue foot, which was hidden from view by giant ice packs. "Yes, Dr Warner."

The old man nodded then shuffled out of the room. Callan squeezed my hand again and I looked over at him. "Thank you for coming to get me."

"I put my number in your phone. Next time, you call me."

"The creek doesn't matter," I said, remembering what he'd said earlier.

Holding my tired gaze, he said, "It does matter, which is why we're going to talk to them."

Unable to fight the pull of sleep, my eyes slipped closed and I mumbled, "I think I like you."

Callan's deep chuckle caressed the room. "About bloody time."

The muffled voices faded, the cool air faded too, and I felt like I was floating, drifting on the edge of sleep.

"I think I could love you."

The words, whispered in dreamland by a smooth voice, warmed my heart as they floated by.

****

Blinking the haze out of my head, I opened my eyes. The dash and front window of Callan's truck filled my vision. My door was swung open, and his steady hands hefted me into his arms. Pushing the door shut with his butt, he rumbled, "Welcome back, baby."

"I slept?" It was a stupid question, but my foggy brain wasn't quite with it.

"Yep. While they put the boot on your foot and until they kicked us out, because they needed the space. Even while I loaded you up and brought you home."

"Home?"

"Yep." His smile sent my tummy into a mad buzz.

A bell jingled and Callan's arms tensed around me.

"Goodness, what happened?" My mother's voice snaked about us, soaking up all the warmth. "Put her down. I'm sure you can walk, Molly."

"She has a broken ankle, Mrs McLean."

"Oh dear."

Callan moved through the door, but Mum was probably right, maybe I could walk. My ankle didn't hurt at all. My head felt super-light though, so maybe being cradled in his arms was for the best. Smiling, I snuggled in close. It felt pretty damn good.

"Where to?" he asked.

"Molly McLean, make that boy set you on your feet."

I reached out and touched the macramé pot, which sent the plant swinging. Callan's mouth kicked up and he raised a brow. Oh right, directions. "Upstairs."

He moved in that direction, his gaze locked on mine. "If you could get the door please, Mrs McLean?"

Raising those gorgeous eyes, he started up the wide stairs, and my mother huffed past us then pushed the door to our quarters open.

I inhaled against his chest, the strong musky smell of him mixed with hay and horse. "Just off the living room, first door on the left."

"For crying out loud, I know your type, Mr Hunter. My daughter is not—"

"Can it, Mum."

Callan's chest vibrated against my side as he chuckled silently. In four huge strides he was across the living space and entering my room, which was filled with stuffed toys and horse posters. My cheeks warmed as he set me on the bed.

"Molly Marie McLean." That was her warning voice, but she could get stuffed.

I reached up to where Callan hovered, cupping his jaw in my palms, and tugged him down. My lips meshed with his, and I kissed the only man I'd ever wanted like my prudish mother wasn't standing right there in my room looking on. Tentative at first, Callan finally matched my enthusiasm, but cut the kiss short when my mother cleared her throat.

"I'll check in on you later." He dropped my bag by the bed, and smiling like he'd just been given a winning lottery ticket, he backed out of my room.

This man had the biggest heart and best smile. Whatever had been holding me back vanished as I realised nothing that had happened between us mattered anymore. He wanted me, and I wanted him right back.

NINETEEN

Not bearing any weight on my foot proved difficult, even with the crutches Callan left in the front office the day he dropped me home. Staying in bed was far less appealing than persevering with the damn things, so it was only two days later before I pulled the wooden contraptions under my arms and swung myself to the top of the stairs.

My phone buzzed against my butt, and smiling, I fished it out of my back pocket. Callan had been texting all morning, mostly stupid selfies of him with Jed. This one though, held only words.

Do you feel like getting out of that place for a bit?

YES!

I'll pick you up in an hour.

A whole hour?

It takes you chicks a while to get ready.

Not this one.

I smoothed my hands over my tie-dyed T-shirt, pushing out the crinkles from lying in bed, then glanced at my reflection in the round mirror which hung by our front door. My hair was tidy, and my cheeks were pink. All was good.

Bracing myself to face the inevitable cold shoulder that my mother would give, I turned the knob on the door and hopped through. Dad glanced up from the front desk, and my entire body sagged with relief. He might have played a part in all the secrets, but ultimately it was her who'd locked me out, then sold me out. I didn't want to be angry anymore, but forgiveness wasn't always easy to give.

"Hi, honey. Are you coming down?"

I nodded, and he pushed up out of the stool, climbing the steps in record time. He grabbed the crutches, leaning them against the counter before returning to slip an arm around my waist. Leaning on him as I hopped down the stairs worked a treat, and when we reached the office I grabbed the crutches. Papers once again littered the desk, all glossy brochures. Dad plopped back into his seat and shuffled them around.

"What's this?" I asked.

"Your eye is just the one I need." He snatched up

a black and pink booklet and flipped it open to a page containing bathrooms. His finger jabbed an image in the centre, the whole room slick and white and ultramodern. "What do you think of this?"

"You're redoing the bathrooms?" I asked.

"Maybe. And we might update all of the decor, paint every room, and give them all fresh carpet."

"Oh." So that's what the creek's sale was funding. I tried to pull an excited smile onto my face. They really did need the money. "Dad, that's going to make such a difference."

He beamed at me. "Regardless of what else happens, I want you to teach me all about this social media stuff the progress committee says I need to conquer. We have to draw in customers before we can keep them coming back."

His excitement seeped into me. "Sure thing. We'll set up a business page on Facebook and a twitter account, maybe an Instagram where we can document the makeover, and—"

He threw up his hands. "Hold on, honey. You lost me."

"Baby steps." I nodded to myself. "I got it."

His gaze cut to the window behind me, and I turned to look over my shoulder. Climbing out of the car she never drove, Mum headed around to the back door and leaned inside.

"Did she tell you Marshall found her high school yearbook?"

His sharp gaze darted back to mine. "No."

"Who's the third wheel? His name was blacked out."

He blew out a sigh, his eyes wandering back to my mother. "That was me."

My tummy dropped. Even though I'd suspected as much, hearing him admit that they weren't the young sweethearts I'd thought hit me like a physical blow.

"She dated Dean Cousins all through the final year of school." He spat out the name as if it were poison.

I waited for him to go on, but my father watched the door, so pulling my phone out of my back pocket, I shot off a text to Callan.

I will need that hour.

Take your time, baby.

Dad still looked outside when I said, "Cousins ... I don't recognise the name."

"They left Bindarra Creek before you were born."

"Oh."

The bell jingled and Mum breezed through, shopping bags hanging off her arms and a huge smile covering her face. "I got some lamps to test out. Whichever one is best we can order over the phone, and they'll get them in to save me another trip to Armidale."

Dad shuffled on the stool. "That's great."

Mum's smile dropped at my father's flat tone.

More shuffling. "It's past time we told Molly the truth."

"The truth." She placed the bags on the ground. "She already knows our plans for the land by the creek."

And as sad as that had made me, it now felt right. Twisting around to look at her, I said, "If you want to sell the creek, I'm okay with. We need the money and ..." I shrugged. "I want to know about Dean Cousins."

Her face paled almost worse than it had done the day I discovered the mystery man of her youth. "How do you know that name?"

"She asked and I told her." Dad walked around the counter and flipped the sign on the front door to *closed*. "Let's go upstairs."

"Please." I hopped that way.

"Patty," Dad said. "Help your daughter."

Mum snapped to attention, dropping the bags she was carrying onto the floor and supported my left side, while Dad took the right. Together, the three of us manoeuvred me up the stairs. It wasn't moving that was difficult so much as lifting the leg covered with a boot that almost reached my knee and made ankle movement impossible. Once at the top, I hobbled over to the couch, careful not to place too much weight on my bunged up foot, and plopped into the comfy lounge. Mum pulled up a chair from the dining table and Dad took a seat beside me, his hand dropping onto my knee.

"Sweetie, sometimes the people you trust most are the ones to let you down."

I edged forward. "What do you mean?"

His throat dipped with a swallow. "Dean pushed me into the dirt in kindergarten. I got up and landed a punch to his gut, but the teacher stopped us before it got any further. We formed some kind of mutual respect and that was it—best mates for life. We were inseparable from that day. We didn't fight again until we were both in the twelfth grade. I stood aside when he decided to chase after my other best friend." Dad's gaze cut to Mum, whose hands twisted around one another where they sat in her lap. "The girl I'd loved since she rode into both our lives on a bay gelding when she was thirteen—"

I glanced across at Mum. "I remember that horse. Brandy, right? His shoe is still sitting in Pop's office ..." Or maybe not anymore.

"That's him," Dad continued. "Your mother had been home-schooled until she reached high school, so neither of us had laid eyes on her before ..."

Mum cleared her throat.

"You're right, Patty; that's another story. They fell for each other pretty hard and I became—as you so aptly put it earlier—their third wheel. That I could cope with; what I couldn't was finding her—"

The screech of Mum's chair on the lino drew Dad's attention.

"I'm sorry. I can't." She fled from the room and Dad retracted his hand from my knee. For a moment I thought he was going to chase after her, but then he twisted to face me on the couch.

He lowered his voice. "After our graduation ball, her parents opened their property to our whole grade for a bonfire. During that after party, I found her sitting in the dust under that huge gum tree out at Bellevue, crying. I slogged him a good one that night, even before I knew what had happened. Weeks later, when she confessed the truth and begged me to take her to the polyclinic, I knew the gut feeling I'd had that night was dead on. Dean was a bastard and deserved a lot more than the one punch I'd given him. You see, they were together, but not sexually. She wasn't ready to give herself to him, but he didn't care. He still took her."

"Ohmygosh." My hands covered my mouth. "How horrible."

"We found out Patty was pregnant that day at the

polyclinic."

He paused, but I didn't need the moment to catch up. "Dean Cousins is my father, isn't he?"

"Yes, honey. But you are *my* daughter."

Staring at the tan squares on the floor, numbness took over.

"And I love you." He pulled me into his hug and my arms automatically closed around him, the man who'd raised me as if I were his own flesh and blood, yet had never let on. I wasn't sure if that made me feel good or bad.

"Why?" I squeaked out. "Why didn't anyone tell me the truth?"

"Your mother can't cope with the truth, Molly. That day we came home from the clinic, right from the start, we told everyone that you were mine. Of course her parents didn't see through the façade. They knew their daughter would never be unfaithful to her boyfriend. She wasn't made of that mettle. It didn't take much for them to figure out the truth."

"But me?"

"Honey, it wasn't anyone's story to tell but hers, and your mother believed she was doing the right thing by letting you grow up in a happy family."

I pushed off the couch, swinging my blue boot around to face the door.

Dad stood too. "It's a lot to take in."

"Yeah, it is."

Hobbling to the door, I tugged it open, and supporting my weight on its handle, swung myself through. The solid timber slammed shut behind me, and dropping to my butt, I slid down the stairs with a series of bumps. My crutches still rested against the counter—a welcome aide to tuck under my arms.

Unlocking the front door, I pushed through it and stood under the awning, waiting for my ride.

Rape was plain horrible and I hated that my mother went through that, but if she couldn't handle a constant reminder then why keep the consequence? A shiver crept up the length of my spine. Worse than an unwanted pregnancy, I was the result of unwanted sex. Leaning against the wall, I slid down it, my crutches clattering to the pavement.

The door beside me swung open and my mother stepped out.

"I'm sorry," she said, slumping beside me.

"I'm sorry, too. That shouldn't have happened to you."

She set her fidgeting hands in her lap. "I don't want you to carry that burden. You deserve a happy life, not being weighed down by my poor choices."

"Poor choices? That guy raped you, Mum. You had no choice."

She twisted her poor fingers so quickly they must have been at risk of knotting up. "Either way ..."

The basher rumbled into the parking space right out front of reception, and Callan stepped out of the ancient beast. Mum stiffened beside me, hostility rolling off her in knots. She climbed to her feet, and I hugged her for the first time in as long as I could remember. "I'm upset you never told me the truth, but I love you, Mum." Her arms tightened around me and I whispered, "Callan isn't Dean. He's a great guy."

She sucked back a deep breath.

"He's kind and caring. Gentle and honest and Mum ..." She stepped back, tilting her head to the side. "I'm pretty sure he'd cross a flooded river to save me. Callan would never hurt me."

"I'll try to trust your judgement, Molly."

"Thank you." I wobbled a little, and she handed over the walking aids.

"Baby," Callan said, stepping forward from where he'd been waiting by the car. "I've missed that sweet smile."

Resting my arms over the crutches, I swung myself forward, and he caught me around the waist. My tummy fluttered in anticipation as he leaned forward, but Callan didn't kiss me. He dipped his chin and said, "Hello, Mrs McLean. Mind if I kidnap your daughter? There's a certain grey giant out at Bellevue pining away for her attention."

"What?" I said. "Horses don't pine."

"Shh," Callan whispered, turning up his smile.

Mum's fingers still worked overtime twisting and turning, but finally, when I thought she was going to say no, she moved toward the office door. "Molly's a grown woman. You'll have to ask her."

Callan winked. "Already done."

"See you later," I shot over my shoulder as Callan landed a kiss on my cheek, nowhere near where I craved it.

The doorbell jingled, and this time his lips met mine, moving softly yet with the pressure of need. His tongue owned my mouth, his lips made mine ache for more, and if it wasn't already kicked up, my left foot would have lifted off the ground. The kiss was that perfect.

Callan was the one to pull away, his lips brushing against mine as he said, "Jed's dying to see you. We'd better go."

"Jed probably hasn't even noticed I'm not there."

Leaving me dizzy, Callan moved to open the car door and took my crutches as I slid into the passenger seat. He tossed them in the back, then ducked around to the driver's side and got in the old basher.

Smiling as I glanced across at him, I realised he was everything I hadn't known I wanted. I settled back into the seat and he started the car, shifting it into reverse. Once we were out on the main road, Callan took his left hand off the wheel and scooped up my right. "Everything okay at home?"

"It will be."

His thumb smoothed over the back of my hand. "If you'd rather talk to me instead of Jed ..."

"It's a long story. Reckon we could ride to the creek?"

"Baby, I'd put money on that huge horse of yours happily carrying us both out there."

"With my ankle?"

Glancing across at him didn't reveal the tilted smile I expected. Instead, Callan's gaze was set on the road ahead. The spot inside my chest swelled, filling the space with its warmth. Riding probably wasn't such a good idea, but the thought of sitting by the creek covered the ache my parents' news had created.

We pulled into Bellevue and they'd been busy in my two day absence. The east paddock looked like a surveyor's workspace, with string lines marking out several quadrants. Callan peeked my way. "I know you love this place and I want what's best for it, and for you. So we're building some cabins in the front. They'll be completely ergonomic, blending in as much as possible, and mostly family-sized. We want people to bring their kids to Bellevue for country getaways. Learn to ride on our gentle horses—which I want you to help me find—take people on trail rides through the back paddock, stopping for damper and fresh tea by the creek, before heading up into the base of the mountains." Callan's eyes sparkled as he pulled up outside the stables. "A family retreat, where people can experience the country horse life. What do you think? Will you allow us to ride through the back paddock?"

"I love it."

Cutting the engine, he scooted out of the car and grabbed my crutches from the back seat. I opened the door, and swung around to climb out. Callan beat me to it. He offered his hand, which I used to pull myself up, then we walked/hopped on crutches into the stables and Jed whinnied at our approach. He actually whinnied, as if he'd missed me.

"Old boy." I patted his nose, then scratched under his chin just as he liked. Callan appeared a few minutes later with a bridle, which he slipped over Jed's ears.

"No way."

"Yes way. You want to visit the creek, then we're visiting the creek."

"What if I come off? It'll kill my ankle."

"Baby, you're not going to come off." He led my horse out into the stables and took the crutches, which he leaned up against the timber wall. With a hand on either side of my waist, Callan hefted me up and I threw my arms over Jed's back, using them to pull myself onto the horse. He tossed the reins over the grey's head, and Jed moseyed forward.

"Hold up," Callan called.

"Catch me if you can." I thought about urging the ex-race horse forward, but the risk of falling off stopped me short.

Smiling, Callan grabbed the reins by Jed's mouth and led the horse to my usual chair, which he aptly used to hoist himself on behind me. Sure arms came around me from behind, taking the leather straps, and he wriggled forward until I was cradled in his thighs. The closeness of his body pressed against mine set off all kinds of tingles inside me.

Jed plodded all the way to the creek. I'd never enjoyed a slow pace so much. When we got there, Callan jumped off the horse and I hoicked my good leg over Jed's side. Strong hands reached up to palm my waist, and Callan bore my whole weight as I slid down. He stopped me from touching the ground, then set me on my feet with gentle care before securing Jed's reins to the usual tree.

I lowered myself onto the grassy bank by the river and a few moments later, Callan's warm body pressed against my side as he settled in beside me. His arm snaked around my waist, and lying back on the slightly sloping bank, he pulled me to him. My heart beat so fast it stuttered, and not waiting a moment longer, I pressed a kiss to the lone freckle on his cheek. Callan's hand cupped my shoulder and he pulled me closer, his lips landing on mine in a kiss that was nothing like the one we'd shared outside the Akuna Motel.

Some time later, the afternoon sun beat down on us as my head once again rested on his shoulder, my leg laid over both of his and my arm curled around his taut tummy. I told him all about Dean Walker and the reason my mother was so jumpy around men. Callan's chest rose and fell under my cheek and it seemed my sharing gates were wide open, because I couldn't stop talking.

"Pop used to love it here. We'd fish off the bank and swim in the creek when the summers were hot. Grandma used to tell him off about the creek water staining my clothes." I smiled to myself. "Yeah, this spot is special, but I really should share the special around. That's why I'm okay with us selling this land to Marshall. Well that, and the fact my parents really need the money."

"Are you sure? Because I think we could persuade Marshall—"

"I'm sure."

Callan's lips brushed the top of my head again, and nestled against his side, I realised maybe home wasn't this property or this creek. Maybe home was the place in my heart that held all the people I loved. Callan hadn't stolen my sanctuary; instead, he'd opened my heart.

EPILOGUE

~three months later~

The glass of my dorm window was cold under my fingertips as I traced patterns over its foggy surface. Armidale sat at the very edges of the unrelenting drought which had plagued Bindarra Creek. Even so, it had been raining here since yesterday and being early April, this was a good sign for the winter to come. Hopefully the low-pressure system had pushed its damp fingers farther west, to my hometown.

"Look at us," Savvy said, sitting on my stripped bed. "Counting down the seconds until we're out of here."

"I know, right?" I didn't move away from the window I'd been staring out for the past half an hour. "College has only been in for a term; you wouldn't think we'd be so keen to get away from each other."

A pillow hurtled across the room, thumping into my chest. "You'll miss me."

My mouth slipped into a telltale smile, but that

didn't stop the taunt falling from my lips. "Not as much as I've missed Callan this term."

"Come on, girl. He practically visits every other weekend. You're not going to see me for an entire three weeks."

"That would be Dane who still acts like an Oxley resident, not Cal."

We both grinned, and I took the three strides to cross my room and wrap my best friend in a hug. With my mouth close by Savvy's ear, I whispered, "I'll miss you like crazy."

Her arms squeezed around me. "We're going to come out your way for winter break. Dane needs the breather, and I'm dying to soak up some of that country goodness that had you glowing after summer."

I chuckled, 'cause that sure wasn't what had me glowing.

A knock on the door made us spring apart. My heart thundered up a storm and my tummy twisted in delight. It felt like so damn long since I'd last seen him. I yanked the door open, and dressed in black and pink designer gym wear, Liv frowned.

"I ..." Her gaze flicked between Savvy and me, as if to weigh up the situation. "I'm glad I caught you both. I just wanted to wish you each a happy Easter. Enjoy your time at home."

She stepped into the room and scooped her arms around us, pulling the three of us together in a group hug. "Love you both."

Savvy's chin pressed against my chest and I yelped. "I love you, too, but you're squishing my boob."

They both laughed and pulled away.

"Who's touching my girl's boob?" A smooth voice

echoed through the hall, and a squeal worthy of Savvy passed my lips.

Callan appeared in the open doorway, and if I thought my pulse had been thundering before then now it roared while doing back flips. With those tailored jeans he practically lived in and a black button-down shirt rolled up to his elbows, the sight of him squeezed my heart. Cal caught Savvy then Liv in his gaze as he rumbled, "Ladies."

Sav shot me a face-splitting smile and ducked out of the room. "Have fun."

Mumbling, "See you after break," Liv followed Savvy into the hall.

I moved close enough to revel in the smell of his musky cologne. Reaching up, I closed my fingers around the neck of his sexy shirt and dragged him down to meet my kiss. Callan's arms swooped around me, and both my feet lifted off the ground as he kissed me back like he'd missed me as much as I had him in the past nine days, seventeen hours, and way too many seconds.

I broke away for long enough to say, "These amazing reunion kisses almost make the time apart worthwhile."

"Mmm. I missed you." Callan kissed the corner of my mouth. "I love you." Soft lips landed on the line of my jaw. "And now you're all mine for three whole weeks."

"Yours and Jed's."

Callan growled low in his throat. "Damn horse doesn't appreciate you."

Pushing away, I swatted his chest and grinning, Cal scooped my backpack off the unmade bed. "Ready to hit the road, babe?"

"More than ready."

I followed him into the hall, and glancing back into my room to make sure I hadn't left anything behind, sighed. Thankfully this was my final year of study, then I'd be free to move away. Yeah, I'd miss the girls something fierce, and Callan and I didn't have solid plans yet, but each time I kissed him goodbye was harder than the time before. Maybe we'd stay in Bindarra Creek and manage Bellevue like Marshall had asked, or maybe we'd do something else. That was the beauty of living in the present instead of the past—anything was possible.

Callan's hand brushed against mine then slipped into my hold, his strong fingers pushing between my own. We traipsed down the two flights of stairs and into the courtyard, where everyone at Oxley loved to loiter, only this morning it was empty as rain fell from the heavens, blanketing the usually sunny space in a heavy mist.

"Wait here," Callan said, as we reached the end of the covered walkway. The parking lot was barely visible, one hundred meters away. He dashed into the pouring rain, making for his huge white truck. Once there, he opened the front door and tossed my bag inside, then pulled something out and over his head.

A picnic blanket? No. The fabric trailed down his back, and as he grew closer I laughed. The strong tang of leather swept around me as he tucked me under the long coat with him.

"You're a real country boy now," I said. "Driza-Bone and all."

Ignoring my quip, he rested a hand on the dip of my back. "Don't run."

Callan directed us into the rain and toward his car.

When we reached it, he tugged open the passenger side, and grabbed my waist to help me inside. No sooner was I seated than the door closed and Cal loped around the front and tossed the wet coat into the back as he climbed in behind the wheel.

The two-hour drive back to Bindarra Creek passed in a heartbeat of loving looks and held hands. By the time we pulled into the driveway of the Akuna Motel I was nowhere near ready to let my honest-to-goodness cowboy out of my sight. He killed the engine and turned to face me, his fingertips brushing my cheek. His lips twitched, curving, and holy crap, just the sight of his mouth was enough to make my tummy perform acrobatics.

"Your mum invited me to dinner, but if you'd rather—"

I slammed my mouth against his lips. My hands crept into the hair at the base of his neck to hold him closer to me, and Callan tugged me across the seat and into his lap. My knees fit around his waist and our mouths connected again. His tongue delved between my lips, massaging mine as he kissed me as if neither of us had any control.

Sometimes I loved this man so much it hurt.

Breathless, I pulled away and grinning, Callan shook his head and opened the door. No rain fell, but the scent of wet dirt filled the air. He deposited me back into my seat, grabbed my backpack and climbed out of his truck. "We'll take this up later."

I jumped down and righted my T-shirt, then ran a hand over my jeans to make sure everything was as it should be. Appearing at my side of the car, Callan pushed the door closed and took my hand.

"Nervous?"

"Not really. Mum and I have had a couple of good chats lately."

"Good." He gave my hand a squeeze and we moved toward the front entrance, which looked decidedly different. The concrete path underfoot was no longer peeling, but rather painted with a fresh coat of glossy grey, as was the timber frame around the glass front door. A gasp escaped me as I pushed through and into the front office, because gone was the hideous carpet and bright orange counter. In its place stood a sleek marble bench top, cream and speckled with shards of grey. The carpet matched everything else. A neutral greyish-green, it was almost the same colour as the rocks that rested in the bed of Bindarra Creek. The Chinese money tree still sat on the counter's corner, but now resided in a lovely shiny black pot.

"Wow."

"You like it, honey?" Dad stood up from behind the desk and moved around to meet me. I threw myself into his hug.

"It's beautiful."

"Thanks to all your advice. Come, your mother's been slaving in the kitchen for hours." He locked up the till and popped a sign on the counter that read, *If office unattended, press bell,* then climbed the stairs that led to our living quarters. Callan motioned that I should go first, which I did.

Pausing at the top of the stairs, I took in everything below. Cal's hand rested on my waist, and as upset as I'd been about the creek, these changes were fantastic.

As if he could read the look in my eyes, Callan said, "Bellevue is doing just as great. And that creek of yours? Marshall and I have a surprise for you."

"You do?"

"Later." He kissed the tip of my nose. "But it might have something to do with a memorial bench."

"I already love it."

And I did, whatever they had planned for the creek, I trusted that Callan wouldn't damage the serenity of the spot. Losing something that I'd held so dear was hard, but the reality was I probably wouldn't have done anything with the land. If I moved back here, it would be to manage the overhauled Bellevue. Yet, Mum's motel had been going under, and her whole life here was in jeopardy. I understood why she'd made the choice she had.

I pushed through the door and into my parents' apartment to be greeted by the sweet scent of Grandma's famous Anzac biscuits. Inhaling the smell from my childhood, my gaze fell on my mother, who hovered over the dining table, teapot in hand.

A rare smile spread across her face. "Are you hungry, Molly? I thought you and Callan might like some afternoon tea."

Returning her warm gesture, I walked across and took a biscuit from the heaped plate. "These smell amazing."

Popping the warm treat into my mouth, I sat in my usual place and motioned for Callan to do the same.

"How was the drive?" Mum asked.

"It rained most of the way." Callan plucked a biscuit from the plate.

"Yes, we had a little here this morning too."

Sitting at my mother's table, with my man's hand resting over the back of my chair, I breathed the first freeing breath I had in a long while.

I forgive you.

I mightn't have said the words aloud, but I meant them. Home was portable. Sitting here with my parents, eating cookies from a recipe I'd baked numerous times with Grandma and eaten just as many times with Pop was just as homely as sitting on the banks of Bindarra Creek, or hugging my best girls back at college.

Home most definitely wasn't a place. It was feeling.

~*~

THE END

Thank you so much for taking the time to read my story ***Stolen Sanctuary*** which is part of the Bindarra Creek Romance series.

~

13 months. 13 authors. 13 romances.

Welcome to Bindarra Creek, a struggling country town where people work hard and love deeply. Set in the picturesque tablelands of New England, Australia, Bindarra Creek is a fictional, drought stricken community full of intrigue, adventure, drama and romance.

Life and love in a small country town has never been more challenging.

Books in the Bindarra Creek Romance series:

For more info on the other stories in this series, please visit

www.bindarracreekromance.com

Want more from Stacey Nash?

Start the Oxley College Saga with Logan and Olivia.

Shh!

What do you do when you're asleep?

Nineteen-year-old Olivia Dean has the perfect reputation, the perfect boyfriend, and an increasingly perfect CV. She has it all, until Christian breaks up with her in public, calling her out as a self-gratifying sexoholic: the kind that plays solo. But Olivia doesn't masturbate all night—the only thing she does is sleep … right?

Now all the boys on campus seem to want her attention for the absolutely wrong reason—including resident hottie, Logan Hays. He's pulling out his best moves to gain her attention, so resisting his sexy charm is hard work. With rapidly slipping grades, a disturbingly lurid reputation and demanding parents, Olivia must discover the truth behind her rumoured sleeping problem. If she doesn't, the perfect life she's worked so hard for may slip away, including the one person who has Olivia breaking all her rules—Logan.

Continue the Oxley College Saga with Savvy and Dane's story.

Pretend...

Life's easy when everything's fake.

Savannah West had it all: popularity, good grades and a family who loved her, but how quickly things can change. Living half a state away doesn't stop the painful memories of her past ripping her heart in two. And sometimes lies are easier than coping with the truth.

The thing she didn't bank on was Dane Beaumont. A blast from her horrendous past, he's the last person she expected to run into at college … and it's not just because he knows the truth. Hot as sin, he's more off limits than generic brand clothing, but staying away isn't easy when he insists on looking out for her. Dealing with the reality of finding her place in the world, Savvy must face the guy who tears down all her carefully placed walls and pull herself together. It's time to grow up.

Read more Oxley College with Jordan and Hex in

Wait!

It's time to play truth or dare.

Jordan Hays knows just how precious life is; that's why he has his own mapped out. He'll work to pay his way through university while he studies hard, regardless of the constant distractions. Because when it comes to becoming a nurse, he's deadly serious. He won't fail to save someone again.

But Hex Penton is way too similar to the sister he lost, and even though the only thing more fun than stupid dares is the crazy girl who sets them, Jordan needs to make a choice. Hex believes every moment is important; every opportunity must be taken, because you never know when the world will be yanked out from underneath you. With the foundations he's based his life on shaken, Jordan must discover what's more important: making sure Hex's life isn't wasted, or remembering how to live his

Acknowledgements

When S.E Gilchrist first approached me about the Bindarra Creek Romance Series I was a little sceptical that I would be able to write a rural romance. Yet, here we are at the end of a story that fit Molly perfectly. My Oxley girl fit into the fictional world that S.E created so seamlessly it's like she was always meant to be there.

Watching this series grow and develop over the period of the past twelve months has been fun, and the authors I've worked with have been an absolute delight. I must extend a warm thank you to each and every one of The Thirteen for making this group series such an easy world in which to play. However, the hugest thank you goes to S.E. Without the endless hours she's donated to the project and the tireless work she does behind the scenes to co-ordinate our little group, this series would not have been what it is. That lady is the bomb! If you ever see her at a signing, an event, or on the street give her a huge smile and tell her how wonderful she is, please.

Lauren McKellar, ST Bende, and Anabel Gonzalez,

thank you once again for being my first readers and amongst my closest friends. You each know just how to bring out the best in my stories and how to push me to be the best writer that I can. Much love. X

My family are the most supportive in the world. From my hubby to my kids to my parents and my best friends, you each put up with unanswered texts, ignored inbox messages, and vacant stares while I'm in the throes of drafting. Thank you for loving me when my creativity takes over and still being there after I write the end.

To my loyal readers and friends, thank you for taking the time to get to know the Oxley crew. After four books, these characters feel so real to me. It warms my heart that other people love them just as much as I do.

Xx

About the author

Stacey Nash calls the Hunter Valley of New South Wales, Australia home. An area nestled between mountains and vineyards, its history and culture have always called to her. Stacey has loved reading for as long as she can remember, so it's no wonder she finally opened a word document and wrote chapter one. Stacey made her publishing debut in 2014 with a young adult novel titled *Forget Me Not*. Writing for the young and new adult market, Stacey's books are all adventure filled stories with a lot of adventure, a good dose of danger, a smattering of romance, and plenty of KISSING!

You can connect with Stacey via

Facebook
Twitter
Goodreads
Instagram

To stay up to date with new releases and upcoming titles be sure to sign up for Stacey's newsletter at the www.stacey-nash.com